The Last Championship

A novella

BRIDGET L. ROSE

The Last Championship

A novella

Bridget L. Rose

This book is dedicated to everyone who thinks they've missed their last opportunity

to reach their dream.

It's never too late.

Try again.

And again.

Until you win.

— Leonard Tick

Trigger Warnings

This book contains vulgar language, explicit sexual scenes, grief, talks of growing a family/having babies, as well as crashes in Formula One that some readers might find scary.

Author's Note

This novella takes place shortly after the end of Jump-Start and the events will continue through the timeline up until halfway through Reserved.

This novella is heavier on the F1 racing (as the title suggests, Leonard is fighting for his last championship), so just be aware of that.

This novella also contains a lot of fluff and no conflict in their marriage, however, there is outside drama to keep things interesting!

To anyone who does not enjoy conversations around growing a family and a couple trying to have children, you might want to steer clear of this one.

Other than that, I hope you enjoy this novella!

Pitstop Series
Team Names

Spark Racing

This is a continuation of Chiara and Leonard's story from *Jump-Start.* Make sure to read their full-length novel first before you read this novella.

Chapter I

Leonard

I t's been almost a whole year since Tim tore down Chiara's art gallery. Since we rebuilt and reopened *Meteorite*. It has been a huge success in all of London. My little demon and I have been... happy doesn't seem like a strong enough word for how it feels to be with her.

I feel whole and utterly at peace.

Six months ago, I asked Mum to give me Grandmum's ring. I already proposed once, but we were both so drunk, all she could do was laugh. The next day, she couldn't remember, and I'd never been more grateful for a hangover in my life because that was not how I wanted our proposal story to go. Chiara deserves a proposal worthy of one of the romance books she's made me addicted to.

"You are such a sap," Graham says as I throw another handful of rose petals on the ground.

"Take notes, Graham. If you ever want Irena to say 'yes' to your proposal, I suggest you become a sap for her, too."

My frown stays in place even as my brother grins at me, clearly very content with my current behavior. Three years ago, I would have never placed rose petals on the ground, leading the way to a picnic blanket with a bouquet of books and roses, food, and champagne. Have a sign with starling birds drawn all over it and the words "Will you marry me?" written in swirls across the blue poster. It's long, almost three meters, but I wanted something grand.

Tonight will be grand.

The sun is about to set, making it the perfect time for Chiara to arrive.

Graham helps me straighten out the picnic blanket once more before shooting me another sly grin and making his way out of *Parco di Monza* to meet my girl at the entrance and blindfold her. I chose the park where we had our first date because I thought it'd be most fitting. We're close to her Nonna and Mamma this way, too, so we can go straight to them and announce that we're engaged.

I know Chiara will love that.

As soon as I see them walking toward me, Graham having covered Chiara's beautiful green eyes with a blue, satin blindfold, my heart lurches in my chest. Even with half her face covered, Chiara is the most beautiful woman I've ever seen.

Ever will see.

Her short, brown hair is perfectly curled, the ends resting on top of her shoulders. The dark blue dress she's put on stops near the middle of her thighs, glittering and reflecting the setting sun's light. The fabric clings to her curvy body, the V-neck cut of the dress dipping low, exposing her cleavage.

I asked her to put on something fancy for tonight because I had a surprise planned. Although she teased me a little, saying she'd wear her best pair of sweatpants, I knew she'd wear something that would make me weak in the knees.

And she did.

Then again, she could have worn the sweatpants, and I also would have been weak in the knees for her.

"I hope this is you finally proposing, Leonard, because if I squeezed my tits into this dress merely for a cute picnic date, I won't let you take it off me later." I almost smile at her pout, at the threatening finger she's pointing at the air beside me. Graham is laughing behind her, which only makes my little demon elbow him in the ribs and frown harder.

I'm not surprised she put it together already. As a matter of fact, I was expecting her to. She's too smart, too observant for me to surprise her with something as big as this proposal. So, the fact that I'm proposing isn't the surprise.

What happens after she says "yes" is.

As soon as my brother stops Chiara in front of me, my hands lift to her elbows, needing to touch her, to feel her skin against mine. I nod at my brother, signaling for him to get the last surprise before my gaze shifts back to my woman. An impatient expression lingers on her lips, and she places her fists on her hips.

"You look absolutely breathtaking, Starling," I say, lifting one of my hands to cup her cheek and run a thumb over those pouty lips.

"I'd tell you how handsome you look, but I can't see shit," she says, making a laugh vibrate off of me.

Carefully, I remove the blindfold, revealing the eyes I fell in love with many years ago. How I ever thought I hated her is beyond me now.

Now, when I've never loved anyone as fiercely and whole-heartedly as I love Chiara.

Now, when she's become my future as well as my present and past.

Now, when I reach for her every single morning in bed, happy when she nuzzles into my side and kisses my jaw.

The mornings I don't spend with her are wasted; the nights we don't make love or cuddle—or both—are empty.

Chiara blinks a few times to adjust her eyes to the fading sunlight, her features softening when she sees me in front of her. A smile tugs at the corner of her mouth as she moves toward me, the world around us blurring into nothing as she steps onto her tiptoes to kiss me. I lower my head, meeting her halfway.

Her peachy scent envelops me, and I revel in it, drinking it in as well as deepening our kiss so all I see and feel is her.

"You do look unbelievable. This outfit—" She cuts off, running a hand down the black button-up I put on. Shivers run down my spine, her smile only intensifying the pleasure of her touch. "It looks so good, it makes me want to tear it right off you." Her hand stops above the button of my pants, her smile turning devious.

"We'll get to that later. First, I have a very important question to as—"

"Yes," she says, cutting me off.

"But I haven't even asked," I argue. Chiara grabs my face in her hands, pulling my lips back down to hers so that when she speaks again, her mouth brushes mine.

"The answer is still yes. Yes, with all my heart, every fibre of my being. It's you and me, Champ, and I want it forever, in every way." My heart aches in the best way, beating too hard and fast. I was nervous she might have changed her mind about wanting to be with me forever. I could not have been more wrong.

I kiss her. Long and deep until we both have to come up for oxygen. Her fingers rub over the short curls at the nape of my neck. Her breaths are shallow, her heart racing as quickly as mine. Her nose glides over mine once before I step back to finally show her the setup of our proposal picnic. Her eyes fall to the bouquet of roses and books, so I pick that up first, handing it to her with a small, unsure smile.

"I bought every copy twice so we can read them together if you'd like," I offer, tears jumping into her eyes when she sees that I arranged the books so the titles spell out "Will You Marry Me?"

"Yes," she replies, her eyes shifting to the sign behind me. I look at it, too, admiring the meteorite painting under the question along with a flock of birds and a trophy for her nickname for me. "Leonard," she gasps, taking a step toward it.

"You have given my life meaning, little demon. You have jump-started my love for racing, my admiration for life, for how valuable it is. You have given me a purpose, a home to run back to after every race. As much as my career means to me, it'll never compare to how much I love you. You fulfill me."

She turns back to me, tears now tracking down her cheeks. I wipe them away even as one drops down my own cheek.

"I love you more and more with every kiss, every touch, every laugh, and every piece of yourself you reveal to me. I want to marry you, and I want forever with you as my wife," I say, dropping onto one knee as I lift the box with the ring up for her. But Chiara drops to her knees in front of me, crying even more now. "And so you'll finally call me 'husband.' That has a much better ring to it than 'Champ' or '*stronzo*,' wouldn't you agree?" That finally makes her laugh again.

"You're ridiculous," she cries and laughs at the same time.

"Yes, ridiculously obsessed with my wife." Chiara flings her arms back around me, burying her face in the crook of my neck as I hug her even closer.

"I love you so much," she says in Italian, but I understand her perfectly. She's said it almost every day for a year.

Once my grandmum's ring is securely placed on her finger, I kiss her again, briefly, just enough to make her melt back against me. Then, a howl comes from the entrance of the park, Benz running toward us with her tongue hanging out of her mouth.

Chiara leaps up, meeting our daughter right before she jumps into her arms.

"Hi, baby! Oh my goodness, what are you doing here?" Chiara asks, hugging Benz.

I'd told Chiara that Benz would stay with my parents while we visited her Mamma and Nonna, but I was planning for Graham to bring her all along.

"It wouldn't be a proper proposal without our daughter here," I explain, watching my wife's eyes shed more happy tears.

Chiara gets lost in Benz for a moment, so I use that opportunity to give Graham the signal for the final piece of the proposal to be released. Once I hit Send on the message, I pick up Benz's leash, holding it tight as I guide Chiara to sit on the picnic blanket beside me.

Then, a few minutes later, a swarm of biodegradable, floating lanterns fill the sky, similar to one of her exhibits at the art gallery. I took inspiration from one of her favorite Disney movies—Tangled—and set this up, pulling out one more lantern I placed behind the picnic basket earlier.

While she's distracted looking at the lanterns, I light up the one in my hand, catching her attention. More tears fall from her eyes, which only makes her slap my arm. It's not hard in any way, but I let out a surprised laugh anyway.

"Hey, what's that for?" I ask while she wipes her tears away.

"For making me cry this much on one of the most beautiful days of my life," she says, her eyes tracing the birds and trophy painted across the lantern as well as the dog paw and the ring. The words "Chiara, Leonard, and Benz (And future babies) Forever" catch her attention. "Why would you do this to me? I hate crying," she says as a sob escapes her. She hugs Benz to her chest, crying even more.

"You have to release it with me, sweetheart. I can't do it alone or it won't mean as much," I explain, so she lifts her hand to the other side of the lantern, keeping eye contact as we raise it and then let go.

"No take-backs now. You're stuck with me," she teases, her tears finally slowing.

"Perfect, because you're stuck with me, too, Chiara."

My lips find hers again, getting lost in the feeling of her, just like I always do.

Like I plan to do for the rest of my life.

CHAPTER 2
Chiara

Mamma, Nonna, Graham, Lulu, and Leonard's mum are in one of my exhibit rooms at the art gallery, helping me put on the finishing touches of my makeup and hair.

Mamma fixes the bow of my dress at the small of my back. Nonna swipes the brush with the blush across the apples of my cheeks, tears in her eyes as she does it. Graham and Rena are sitting on the couch, my best friend is fixing my flower bouquet based on his mother's advice.

Nonna glides the brush over my skin one final time before a tear finally falls down her cheek.

"When Leonard came to us to ask for our blessing to marry you, I tried to picture this day. I tried to envision how beautiful you'd look in my dress, but nothing I came up with compares to reality."

She takes a step back, taking my hands and lifting them to admire the way her dress fits me. We had it altered; cut off the sleeves and tightened the chest area. The dress is princess-style with a layer of lace that has birds woven into it covering it entirely. It was a new addition Nonna insisted on. She said, "I want the birds to make Leonard cry." I almost fell over laughing.

"You are a vision," Mamma adds, hugging me from behind. Nonna wraps her arms around me from the front until we're standing in the middle of the room, hugging for a very long time. "Did you have to grow up so quickly?" my mother adds, squeezing me one last time before releasing me again.

My beautiful Nonna grabs my face, kissing each of my cheeks.

"Your Nonno and Papa would have been so proud of the woman you have become, for fighting for your dream career but also for loving as strongly as you do." My hands run over the birds on my dress as tears jump into my eyes, but she pinches me to keep me from ruining my makeup. "None of that. Your makeup is done, so you're not allowed to cry," she scolds, making a low laugh escape me.

Mamma and Nonna turn to the vanity to do their makeup when I hear Rena calling out to me. I grab the front of my dress, lifting it a little to keep from stepping on it. Graham rushes toward me, adjusting my train so I don't trample on that either. Once I'm settled down on the seat beside Rena, she searches for my hand, one of hers curled into a fist.

"I have something for you," she says, lifting her palm to reveal a necklace lying on it. The charm hanging from it is a simple silver plate with raised dots on it. I recognize it as Braille instantly.

"What does it say?" I ask, my voice soft and void of all strength, grabbing the charm and running my fingers over it.

"To my daughter, I love you as brightly as the stars in the sky." She searches for the necklace again, so I hand it back to her, letting her feel her way to my neck where she reaches around to open the clasp and close it at my nape. The necklace falls against my sternum, the material warm from us holding onto it.

"I love you, too, Rena. So much," I reply, pulling her into a hug.

A moment after everyone but Graham and Lulu leave, my best friend since childhood and my oldest friend turn to me. Graham gives my chin a small nudge.

"If you're expecting any sweet words, you won't get them from me. The only thing I can offer you is my deepest condolences," he teases, a half-smile tugging on the corner of his full lips. He looks so much like Leonard, only younger and with fewer tattoos.

"I don't want words. Where's my gift? I got something from Mamma, Nonna, Lulu, and Mum. Leonard said I'll get his gift later. So, the only person left is you," I say, wiggling my brows at him. He places his hands on his hips in challenge while Lulu snickers, the earrings *I* gifted *her* dangling from her lobes already.

"Oh yeah? And where is my gift?" he asks. I let out a "pfft" as I walk toward my bag, pulling out a small gift for him.

"As my man of honor, do you really think I wouldn't have a gift for you?" I say as I hand him the box.

"No, don't do this to me. I don't have a gift for you! Now I just feel like an arse," he says, rubbing his hands over his handsome face. Lulu bursts into laughter.

"I told you to get her the bikini set we were looking at. She could have used it for her honeymoon," Lulu replies, carefully shifting her black hair over her shoulder to let it rain down her back.

"And I told you I didn't want to buy her something my brother would have most likely ripped to shreds the second he saw her in it." I would argue, but Leonard has broken more panties than I could count. He always buys me two the day after as replacements, but they don't last very long either.

"I was teasing, Graham. I don't want anything from you. I do, however, want you to open my gift. I want you to wear it," I reply, biting on my bottom lip to keep from smiling.

"I hate you." He opens the box and takes out the keychain I got him. It's the cutest, most disgustingly cliché charm that has our names on it and says "BFFs." "God, this is horribly cliché, Chiara," he says before adding, "I love it," and hugging me. "I still don't have a gift for you," he mumbles against the side of my head.

"You organized this entire day, Graham. You, Lulu, and Jack outdid yourselves, and I'll never be able to repay you," I say, holding onto the hug for a moment longer and smiling at Lulu over Graham's shoulder.

"Your husband was the brain behind all of this. It was his vision," he says and steps back, one of his hands remaining on my shoulder.

"Yes, and thank goodness for that because I didn't want to be in charge," I reply, laughing a little as I say the words.

"You look so happy," Graham adds after a moment of silence while he studies my features.

"Leonard makes me happier than I've ever been."

Graham is about to respond when first his phone rings and then the door slams open, Adrian Romana stepping through it with a wild look on his face. He's wearing a black-on-black suit with the top three buttons of his shirt undone to reveal the chain of a necklace. He ditched his suit jacket and rolled up his sleeves to expose his trained forearms. Rings cover his long fingers, and as he steps into the room and closes the door, he raises one hand, showing them off.

"We don't have a lot of time. I can sneak you out of here, but we have to leave in two minutes. Otherwise, he'll catch us," Adrian says, his face all serious even though I know he's kidding.

"Leonard will kill you if he finds out you said that," I remind him, but he merely gives me an unbothered, seductive smirk.

"How would he find out?" I turn to Graham, noticing his phone in his hand, Leonard's name on the screen from a phone call. My best friend hits Speaker and a second later, Leonard's voice fills the room.

"Because I always find out. Now, step away from *my wife* and meet me in my room so I can break your pretty face," Leonard says, his voice low, threatening.

"You thinking I'm pretty is all I needed to hear today." Adrian winks at me, then adds, "Seriously, though, if you need to escape, say the word. I'm your guy." He leaves again, and Graham lets out a booming laugh.

"If I were you, I'd take that offer. Adrian's incredibly hot," he says, so I nudge his side.

"Leonard is the love of my life, Graham, and I'm his. Adrian has yet to find his person." And I'm looking forward to watching him fall all over himself for someone.

"I could be his person," Lulu says with a wiggle of her brows. "At least for a night," she goes on before stepping out of the room.

Graham and I exchange one more smile before I run my hands over the front of my dress.

"I'm ready to finally walk down the aisle. I've waited long enough."

"So have I," Leonard replies, and I flinch visibly when I realize Graham didn't hang up.

"God, you scared me," I say with a laugh, taking the phone out of my best friend's hand to talk to him.

"I'm sorry, sweetheart, I didn't mean to. Come kiss me so we can be husband and wife on paper as well as in our hearts." He wants us to be tied together in every way, him belonging to me and me to him.

And I want that, too.

"On my way."

Leonard, Jack, Lulu, and Graham outdid themselves. *Meteorite* is covered in flowers with benches for our family to sit on in front of the altar. Nonna, Mamma, Graham, and Lulu are already standing on my side of the altar while Jack, Stu, Ellie, Quinn, and Adrian are on Leonard's side.

Benz sits beside her daddy, whose eyes entirely fixated on me the second I step into his line of vision. I can't look away from him either. He's wearing a blue suit, his dark, tattooed skin perfectly complemented by the color. His hair is cut shorter again, his stunning curls on full display for me. His brown eyes, my favorite set in the world, fill with tears at the sight of me, but he takes a deep breath to keep them at bay.

But the most beautiful thing about him is the bright smile shining my way. Smile lines are on either side of his mouth, somehow making him even more handsome than he already is.

Our daughter's tail starts wagging as soon as she sees me, but she's so well-trained, she stays next to Leonard even as I walk toward them.

"Don't trip, don't trip, don't trip," I mumble to myself, but I think Leonard knows exactly what I'm saying because he takes a step toward me, asking if that's what I need. If he's what I need. I nod without hesitation.

Leonard meets me halfway, his hands finding my forearms so he can steady me. My knees almost wobble when he's finally touching me.

"Thank you," I whisper, holding onto him, too. "This dress is not made for walking," I explain, reveling in the warmth of his touch and smile.

"You are so breathtaking, sweetheart, there are no words that can describe just how beautiful you are." His eyes rake over my body again, the tears returning to his eyes.

"So are you," I reply, both of us completely forgetting there are people waiting for us to make our way to the front where Leonard's father is waiting to marry us. Andrew gives me a small nod, grinning to himself.

"I really want to marry you," Leonard says, bringing my attention back to him.

"Then help me walk to the front," I reply, tugging on my dress again. Leonard smiles, pressing a swift kiss to my lips before leading me toward his father.

I'd be lying if I said I hear much of what Andrew says. I'm too entranced by Leonard. By the way he looks at me. By the way his eyes feel like they caress every inch of my face as he traces my features. By the way his hands cling to mine.

My mind only starts working again when it's time for our vows. Leonard opens his mouth to start, but I cover his lips, making everyone chuckle.

"I'm sorry, but I have to speak first because we both know I'm nowhere as good with words as you," I say, feeling him pressing a kiss to my palm. I lower my hand again, watching an amused expression spread across his face. "From the day you destroyed my sandcastle and I shoved your face into the remains, I knew you and I would be tethered together forever. I think neither one of us knew what to do with the connection we felt, so we decided hate would be easier than addressing these feelings."

His eyes soften a little at my words, making him drag me closer.

"I was so stubborn, and so were you, but I'm so grateful you were less so than I am. That you fought for me, for us. That you let me into the sanctuary of your soul and gave me a home. Thank you for fighting *with* me, for giving me the strength to keep going when all I wanted was to fall apart. Thank you for showing me parts of you that you've never shown anyone else, that you won't ever show anyone else."

My voice quivers, so Leonard squeezes my hands where they rest in his.

"We were both so set on never falling in love, and yet, neither one of us ever truly had a choice, did we?" I ask. Leonard shakes his head without hesitation.

"Not even a little." His forehead drops to mine, resting there for a moment.

"I love you. I've loved you for so long, and I'll love you even when we're ghosts and haunting our children for shits and giggles," I add, hearing everyone laugh in response, including Leonard. "I am yours, even in death. Even when I no longer have lips to love you with, I'll still find a way to speak the words." Leonard's mouth is on mine a second later, kissing me while I giggle. I hear someone whistling, without a doubt Adrian, making Leonard smile, too.

"I should have fought to go first," Leonard says as I wipe my finger over his lips to remove my lipstick. He grabs my wrist, kissing it and stopping me. "Chiara," he starts. "Starling." His eyes sparkle with joy. "Little demon." He takes a deep breath for courage. "My sweetheart, you are *everything* to me. I've won two World Championships with Grenzenlos, but the best day of my life will forever be the day you told me you love me. The day you gave yourself to me in the same way I gave myself to you."

One of his hands finds the area above my heart.

"You are unlike anyone else I've ever met. You are a fighter, so strong and resilient. You've beaten up more people for fun than I can remember. You've fought more battles emotionally than anyone ever should have. But even through the pain, you've always grown stronger. It's something I admire more than I'll ever be able to express."

His hand travels upward, cupping my cheek.

"*You* taught *me* how to be strong. How to love someone the right way. Uncon-ditionally. Passionately. Wildly. Marrying you today doesn't just mean you'll be my wife. You've been my wife in my head since we started dating because I knew there was only one direction I wanted us to go. I wanted us to get here, to today. Marrying you today means my dream comes true. It means something I never wanted to do with anyone before you, that became all I wanted, finally being mine." Leonard drags me against his chest, his nose rubbing over mine. "Next dream: enjoying life with you, then expanding our family when we're ready."

He kisses me again, but this time, he doesn't pull back, and I don't want him to either.

Andrew calls out that he officially announces us husband and wife, our whole family clapping happily for us.

"I love you, *amore*."

"I love you so much, sweetheart," he replies quickly, obviously eager to get back to kissing me.

And I kiss him back just as passionately.

CHAPTER 3
Leonard

As a wedding present, I bought Chiara an island in Italy. It's small for an island, but she still looked at me with a dropped jaw, shock paralyzing her body.

It took her a minute to process that piece of information before she mumbled something along the lines of, "Two years ago I didn't have clothes without holes in them, now I own an island. That's fine. Totally normal."

Then, she turned to me and, seeing my smile, burst into laughter. She jumped into my arms, attacking my lips with hers while I carried us inside our villa. We spent the rest of the night making love, slow and softly. Our emotions ran so high, neither one of us wanted anything else. We just wanted each other, as close as possible, for the first time as husband and wife.

We went swimming today with Benz, who is now passed out on the dog bed I had brought here months ago when I bought the island and had the villa renovated. Chiara and I also spent a lot of time reading, kissing, eating, and sleeping.

She went to take a shower half an hour ago, and I've been patiently waiting in our bedroom with my guitar sitting on my lap, playing random chords I think sound good together. I hum a melody to go along with them when the bathroom door opens again, my little demon stepping into our room in a lingerie set that would bring me to my knees if I were standing. It's blue and entirely made of lace with a garter belt. Her thong is barely covering her, and her bra is see-through.

I place my guitar on the floor, my skin on fire. My cock hardens in an instant, begging me to get to her.

I should have known she'd have something planned for me.

"Wait," she says, her hands behind her as she leans against the wall next to her.

I stop immediately, waiting very impatiently for her instructions. I love it when she takes control, even if I really want to throw her over my shoulder and carry her to the bed right now to pull her thong to the side and drive into her.

"Get on your knees for me, husband," she instructs, not moving an inch, merely watching me with lust. Her eyes drop to my hard cock, which is only covered by my tight boxers.

I obey without hesitation.

"Good boy," she praises. "Now, crawl to me," she goes on, her voice even and firm.

Again, I don't hesitate. I get on all fours and crawl to her, watching her push off the wall to meet me halfway. My hands snake around her legs as soon as I'm in front of her, my lips finding the top of her thigh.

"What do you want? Tell me, and I'll give it to you," she says, her fingers running through my curls.

"I want to push this excuse of underwear aside and have you sit on my face until you scream my name," I reply, running my hands over her perfect arse before squeezing it.

"Tell me more. I want you to describe it, and if I like what I hear, I'll let you take control," she says, licking her lips as she looks down at me.

"I want to bury my tongue inside of you, flick it over your pretty clit until you're coming all over my mouth. I want you to grind down on me and ride out your orgasm, screaming so loud, all of Italy knows how good I make you feel," I say, pressing a soft kiss to her stomach. "Then, I want you to crawl down my body and ride my cock, fucking me however you want to. Using me because you know how much I love it when you use me, sweetheart."

Her eyes flicker with heat. Goosebumps trail over her arms as she brings her hand to my chin, cupping it as she lifts my gaze to meet hers.

"I want all of it," she says, her voice low and thick with desire.

I'm on my feet a second later, guiding Chiara to the bed with a kiss so consuming, I hardly feel it when we tumble onto the mattress, her mouth still on mine. My hands roam over her garter belt, the rough fabric bringing a smile to my face.

"This stays on," I say, running my hands over her thighs again where the belt connects with the garters. "But the bra, baby, *that* needs to disappear. I want to worship your breasts," I say, practically beg, but my tease of a wife takes her sweet time removing it.

Her hands slip over her breasts first, pinching her nipples through the fabric. She moans, grinding against the thigh she's straddling. My cock gives a needy throb, and I have to grip the sheets to keep from grabbing her hips and placing her on top of my dick so she grinds against it instead. Chiara rolls her hips again, her pussy so hot and wet, I can feel it against the bare skin on my thigh. My control snaps, so I grab her hips and bring her all the way to my face, my back flat on the mattress as she now straddles my head.

"That's much better," I say as Chiara giggles on top of me, still removing her bra. "Can I taste you, sweetheart?" Her answer is her hand dropping to her pussy, guiding her panties to the side, and exposing herself to me.

My lips find her clit a breath later, hearing her moan for me and watching her tremble on top of me. I hold onto her thighs, steadying her as I flick my tongue over her pussy, enjoying how fucking wet she is for me.

I'll never get tired of how much it turns her on when I obey her every command.

"Hold onto the headboard," I instruct, watching her lift her arms to the wooden piece before I continue playing with her pussy.

Chiara rolls her hips in harmony with my licks, chasing her orgasm as I slip my tongue inside of her and back out to play with her clit.

"Oh, fuck, Leonard! Fuck, shit," she moans, screaming my name when I suck on her clit, making her see stars. "I'm so close, please don't stop," she begs, her hand grabbing onto my curls and tugging as she fucks my face harder and faster. I hold onto her, letting her chase her pleasure and enjoying the taste of her as she drips all over my mouth.

I could eat Chiara out for days and never get tired of the moans, of the way she screams my name in pleasure.

My hand slips between us, gliding over my stomach and toward my cock. I give it a rough jerk, trying to relieve the pressure that's been building since Chiara walked out of the bathroom. I moan against her pussy, making her shake on top of me. My tongue dips inside of her again right before her hands fall back onto the headboard while she grinds against my mouth and screams my name. I fuck my hand, desperate for a release too because there's nothing hotter than Chiara coming all over my face.

Except when she comes on my cock.

Or hands.

Or by herself while I watch.

I kiss her swollen pussy two more times, letting her come down from her high and stroking my cock gently. My entire body is on fire, needy for her walls to be wrapped around me.

"You're so beautiful when you come, sweetheart," I say, pressing kisses along the inside of her left thigh.

"Your mouth is magic," she says with a little moan, her eyes still closed as she cups her breasts, then runs her hand upward and into her hair.

"So is your pussy, Chiara. Come wrap it around my cock," I say, making a smile take over her whole face. She crawls down my body, licking her hand before wrapping it around my cock and forcing a low groan from my lips.

Her lips find mine, a whimper escaping her when she tastes herself on my lips. She loves it when I'm covered in her, marking me as hers. She loves leaving more visible ones, too. Scratching my back. Hickeys. Fucking me so hard we both walk a little funny in the morning.

I love every bit of it.

She strokes me a few times, humming happily into my mouth as she guides my cock to her entrance and then sinks down on me completely. For a moment, the pleasure is so intense that my limbs go weak and my head falls backward onto the pillows.

"Fuuuuck," I moan, my fingers digging into her thick thighs. "You feel so good, so wet for me," I croak out as she rolls her hips, grinding her clit against my pelvis.

"You're so hard for me, husband. Tell me," she starts, lowering her mouth to my ear while continuing the slow rolling of her hips. "Was it crawling toward me or having your face buried between my legs?"

Her hard nipples graze my chest as she rides me, my body on fire from her teasing. I grab her arse, squeezing it hard before lifting Chiara off me only to push her down again, driving upward simultaneously. She cries out, gripping the sheets beside my head so hard, her knuckles turn white.

"All of it, Chiara. It was all of it," I say, flipping us around because I'm too impatient to let her keep teasing us.

Another giggle leaves her as I turn us over, but it dies out as soon as my mouth wraps around her nipple, sucking hard. I work my way upward while my hand wraps around my dick to guide it back inside her. With my mouth hovering over hers, I thrust into her wet paradise, keeping eye contact with her as we both moan.

"I'm yours. Your husband. Forever." I fuck into her hard and fast, driving us closer to our orgasms. "And you're mine. My wife. Forever. This is mine forever," I say as I stroke her clit in tight circles that make her walls squeeze my cock.

"All yours," she replies with a lust-filled smile.

I go back to playing with her nipples, my movements picking up speed because I'm close. I'm so fucking close, but so is Chiara. Her nails dig into my back as her legs wrap around my hips, pulling me closer.

My orgasm explodes through me, setting off fireworks behind my eyes. I groan while Chiara screams through her high, squeezing every last drop of cum out of me by tightening her walls around me. I almost collapse on top of her as wave over wave of pleasure crashes through me, a feeling of pure ecstasy lighting my cells on fire.

"I don't think I'll ever get tired of this," Chiara says, her thumb trailing over my bottom lip. I kiss her finger, then her mouth before slipping out of her and kneeling in front of her. I watch my cum drip out of her while she smiles at me.

"I don't think I'll ever get tired of this sight," I reply, guiding my finger over her pussy and admiring the way she's dripping with me.

I know she's on birth control and the likeliness of her getting pregnant is very low, but for a split second, I imagine her round belly. I imagine us expanding our family. Despite what many people believe, and something I've realised more recently, Chiara and I are already a family. Just her and me. And Benzie, of course. Children don't make us a family. We'd merely have a bigger one, more members to love with our whole hearts. And I don't just want kids to grow our family. I want more dogs. I want to let Adrian, Cameron, hell, even Valentina, in and grow our family through friends. Having kids is simply something we both want. I want my child to break barriers. I want to teach them to never give up, to fight for their dreams. I want to give them the opportunities I had to bleed for.

I want—

"Holy shit," I say, an idea blooming to life in my head.

"What is it?" Chiara asks, pushing up to place her weight on her elbows. A bright smile spreads across my face, so I kiss her, disappearing into the bathroom to grab a wet towel.

"They've been introducing driver academies over the last few years, giving young racers the opportunity to train there. But they're still giving most of these opportunities to privileged, white boys. Not to women. Not to people of colour. Not to kids whose parents can't afford to put so much money into their futures. I want to change that. I want to open my own academy and give opportunities to..." I trail off, searching for the right word as I clean Chiara up.

She watches me, a slow smile stretching her full lips wide.

"Kids like you," she finishes my sentence. I nod several times, my chest warming at her words.

"Kids like me," I confirm, the idea consuming my mind piece by piece. I shake my head to refocus on Chiara, a little scared she'll be upset where my thoughts have gone after we just had sex, but I find her grinning at me instead. "What?" I ask, rubbing my hands down her legs.

"Your mind, it never ceases to amaze me. You constantly try to find ways to make this world a better place, and I want you to know I love you all the more for it," she says, shaking her head before dropping back down on the mattress.

I remove her panties, garter belt, and garters before sliding down my boxers and lying down beside my wife. She drapes her body over mine, her heated skin pressed against mine. My forehead drops to hers while I trace the area on her hip where her skin is lighter because her bathing suit covered her when she was tanning. Chiara uses her finger to trace every line of my tattoos she can find.

"You'll need a partner," she says. "Someone who's experienced a similar type of discrimination as you in the world of motorsport. Someone who's going to be just as passionate as you about this project. Finalize this idea, then find your partner."

As always, she's absolutely right.

"I have someone in mind."

CHAPTER 4
Leonard

Grenzenlos is battling Hawke Racing for both the Drivers' Championship and the Constructors' Championship. There are two races left, and I'm five points ahead of my rival, Rick Sennon. My team is only leading by eleven points over Hawke.

Jonathan, the absolute useless piece of work that he is, has been slacking the entire season. He went from being my rival to barely making it into the top ten. He claims my car is simply faster, but we both know his mind's been somewhere else for the last eight months. I wouldn't judge him for it, would understand, if I didn't see him out partying every weekend. It's as if he gave up on trying to become a champion after the second time I beat him last year. It's sad, but I don't have time to deal with someone who's been an arsehole to me from day one.

I'm too busy being happy.

With Chiara's gallery being a huge success, she's decided to join me for the last few races of the season. We've been married for almost a year now, and it's safe to say that I've never felt so much joy in my whole life. We've traveled a lot, spent more time on our island—which I insisted we call "de Luca" for her last name since I replaced it with mine when we got married—and redecorated our apartment. We've also been playing with my driver academy idea, so I've spent quite some time trying to figure out how to set it in motion as well.

"Alright, Tick, I've got a challenge for you," Adrian Romana says as he walks over to where I'm standing with my team in the middle of the track, discussing strategies and track conditions for the race weekend here at the Losail Circuit in Qatar. He's holding two sets of in-line skates, some padding, and two helmets.

"This can't be a good idea," I say, shaking my head. "You do understand I have a race in four days, one that might just decide if I win the championship or not." It's not likely, but, it's a possibility. So, I really shouldn't be reckless.

Then again, I found out almost two years ago that "should" and "will happen" are very different things when it comes to Adrian Romana.

"Nonsense. This is a fantastic idea. It'll be fun," he replies, flashing me one of his cocky smirks and offering me the in-line skates in challenge.

"For who? You or me?" The corner of my mouth twitches, but I fight back a smile.

"For me. You may have the faster F1 car, but I'm quicker than you," he replies, dropping onto the floor to put the skates on. I can't help it. I let out an amused chuckle.

"We'll see about that," I say, sitting down as well to put on my skates.

A minute later, once we're both clad in the protective gear and in-line skates, my team and Adrian's spread out, acting as the start and finish line. There are maybe five hundred meters between them, enough to kick his arse before I continue with my day.

Although, I *am* a bit nervous because Adrian's a head taller than me, and his legs are longer, which may give him an advantage. Quinn, my best friend and performance coach, stands in front of us with a megaphone in her hand.

"Where the fuck did you get that?" Adrian asks with a delighted laugh.

"I have my ways," she replies and winks at him before turning to our teams and announcing, "Welcome, everybody, to the first annual in-line skate race between two idiots—I mean, two Formula One drivers." I frown at Quinn while Adrian snickers.

"Can we get on with this?" I ask, adjusting my elbow padding and helmet. My best friend gives me a grin before counting down aloud for Adrian and me.

"GO!" she screams through the megaphone, but Adrian already started a split second before she said the word.

"Hey, jump start, you cheater!" I call out as I skate after him, catching up to the Monegasque. Once I'm close enough, I use my body weight to somewhat *gently* shove him toward the curb and slow him down.

"You dickhead!" Adrian says when he has to slow down and stumbles over the curb and onto the gravel.

I make it to the finish line with him far behind me, celebrating my victory by flipping him off. Adrian bends over at the waist as he bursts into laughter.

"What the hell was that?" he asks through wheezing sounds.

"Nothing, just an incident," I reply, and suddenly, we're both laughing.

My team gives me weird looks because this is the first time I've ever laughed in front of them, but I don't care right now.

I keep going until Adrian and I are both keeled over, our stomachs cramping.

"Next time, let's try scooters," Adrian says once we've both recovered enough to speak.

"You're so on."

My heart is racing as if this is the first time in my life I'm so close to getting a championship title. My breaths are coming out shaky. My limbs are heavy with fear. Normally, I have a good grip on my nerves. I've been doing this for over twenty years. Racing comes as naturally as breathing, and yet, I feel like I'm about to have a panic attack. It's an awful, dreadful feeling, which is why I take another moment to hold onto Chiara before I have to warm up and get into my car to start the race.

I qualified second yesterday, a mere two-hundredths of a second slower than Rick.

"You are amazing. In every single way. I believe in you." She gives me more encouragement that I drink in without hesitation, enjoying the way it feels to have her unconditional faith. Even when we thought we hated each other, Chiara always believed in my ability to achieve great things.

"Without you, none of this would mean a thing." Her lips brush mine, but she pulls back quickly, digging around in her pocket to take out my wedding ring. I gave it to her this morning because all drivers have been forbidden from wearing jewellery during race weekends. She slides it on top of her ring, then places her palm right above my heart.

"No matter what, Benzie and I will be here, cheering you on, always on your team." I step back a little, tugging strands of hair behind both of her ears before cupping her cheeks.

"I don't know what I'd do without you, sweetheart," I say, caressing the apples of her cheeks. "I hope you still know that I'd give you the world. I'll forever place it at your feet, Starling."

"You're my world," she whispers, her fingers snaking around my wrists. "Come back to me in one piece. That's all I'll ever need."

Her words ring in my ears long after I'm in the car, getting ready to start the race. The scent of burning rubber fills my nose, sending a wave of adrenaline through me. Engines rev, fans scream, and my body hums with anticipation. I try to ignore the way my hands shake, dread filling my stomach.

Something's wrong today. I can't put my finger on it, but I feel off. Like something bad is about to happen.

The feeling distracts me, and I barely snap out of it in time to watch the lights disappear and Rick's car shoot forward. I follow behind him, but my reaction time's off. He makes it through the first corner without a threat from me while I still try to fight past that strange feeling in my chest.

It's so hot.

Sweat drips down my back. The heat is unbearable, especially combined with the exertion of using every single muscle to race. I don't know why they decided to do the Qatar Grand Prix at the end of the season. The cars turn into saunas, slowly burning the drivers inside.

Tire degradation is awful.

I struggle to keep up with Rick. My hard tyres lose grip only ten laps into the race. Every muscle in my body feels strained.

There is no way I'm winning this race today, but I push anyway. If I can't be first, I have to stay second or Rick will overtake me in the championship standings.

But I have to fight hard. My seat is a heated piece of metal. Sweat trickles from my forehead into my eyes. It feels like I'm getting burned alive halfway through the race, but when I talk to Riley, my race engineer, about it, I get no answer that helps me. They tell me every driver is going through the same thing, to keep pushing until the end.

After the second pitstop, Rick and I are close together. Blinking through the burning sensation of sweat hitting my eyes, I use all of the strength I have left to close the gap between us.

I'm in DRS range. I get a speed advantage down the main straight, but it's not enough to help me overtake yet. I see black spots in my vision, my body suddenly featherlight. A dizzy spell hits me hard, so I back off attacking him, fighting back the overwhelming nausea.

"Leonard? What's happening?" My race engineer's voice is so far away. I can hardly hear them.

"I feel…I'm gonna—" I cut off, pressing my lips together and humming to keep the nausea at bay.

"Talk to me, Tick."

"Pass out or throw up," I finish, the words coming out quickly.

"Six laps to go. Push through it, man. You can do it. I'm so sorry." It's not their fault at all, but the encouragement does nothing to help me. Riley and I haven't been working together very long, but I like them. They're nice and smart, but I kind of want to cuss them out right now for sitting in the garage with their little fan.

Somehow, I make it over the finish line without doing either of the things I warned my race engineer about. I come in second, but I don't even care anymore. I'm just so tired.

Without realizing or processing much of what happens, I drive my car to the second place sign, turning off the engine and sitting there for a second until the nausea returns. I rush out of the car, spotting the medical vehicle off to the side.

My legs hardly work and I almost fall to the ground when I'm on my feet.

I spot Rick getting out of his car, falling against the side of it to keep from dropping to the floor, too.

Fuck.

The other drivers must feel the same as me.

I rip my helmet off using the last bit of energy I have left and stumble over to the medical crew.

"I need help," I say, pulling off my balaclava.

The paramedics rush toward me, the fans and crews silent as the black dots return to my vision until they take over completely, the world disappearing into nothingness.

The last thing I hear is my wife screaming my name.

CHAPTER 5
Chiara

"Listen, I have had enough. They didn't let me ride in the ambulance with him, didn't even let me see him. There was an accident on my way here to the hospital, so I was stuck in goddamn traffic for half an hour. My patience isn't just running thin, it has run out." I lean onto the desk, toward the man I'm addressing. "I'm a trained fighter, and I have no problem kicking my way through every fucking person in this hospital that keeps me from getting to my husband."

The nurse sitting at the front desk of the hospital leans a bit away from me, his eyes going wide and his lips parting. I'd feel bad if he hadn't told me, "It may be difficult to understand for *you*, but without proper marital documentation, I cannot give out patient information." Okay, maybe I feel a little bad considering he's practically pissing himself now, but not nearly enough to stop my fear from turning into more frustration and anger.

Plus, he practically insinuated I'm stupid, so he had this coming.

"I don't keep my fucking marriage license on me, and I haven't had the chance to change my name on my passport or driver's license. But I am Leonard Tick's wife. And you will let me see him," I say, feeling a comforting hand slip onto my shoulder. Quinn, Leonard's performance coach and a very good friend of mine, squeezes once before handing me a piece of paper.

"Copies of all your documentation," she says and nods reassuringly.

"What kind of a shit hospital even asks for this?" I mumble under my breath, hearing Quinn chuckle quietly beside me.

"You do realize it's not his fault, yes?" Quinn asks after the nurse starts looking over the files.

"I understand, but I still don't like him." I shoot the nurse a threatening glare, and he immediately hands me back my documents.

"Room 2A, ma'am."

Quinn and I speed toward the elevator, rushing to get to Leonard. I think about Benz for a moment, hoping she's okay with Adrian, but then the doors slide open and I focus on getting to Leonard. Benz will be fine. Adrian took her leash and practically danced out of the room with her. Well, as much as someone who almost passed out from the heat and exhaustion of the Qatar Grand Prix could.

Leonard isn't the only one that fainted. One of the Spark Racing drivers fell to the ground after getting out of his car and didn't get up anymore. Cameron Kion threw up in the nearest trash can. Jonathan Kent couldn't even get out of his car. More drivers struggled with the heat, so many that the press conference after the race and most of the other interviews were canceled. Some of the other drivers were also taken here, to the hospital where they brought my husband.

"He'll be alright," Quinn assures me, and, while I logically agree with her, it feels like a part of me has been swimming in darkness since I watched Leonard fall to the ground earlier.

His crew held me back from getting to him, but my heart sank at the sight of my man, the one who's always so strong and put together, even after crashing during a race weekend, crumbling to the floor. I hated the people in charge for doing something like this to all of the drivers. I hated them for letting it go on even after so many of them radioed in that they weren't feeling well.

I understand people paid a lot of money to watch the race, that there would be fans who wouldn't understand, but the well-being of the drivers *always* has to come first. Without question. Without argument.

My husband should not be in a fucking hospital bed right now because they didn't stop the goddamn race!

My legs shake, but I run to him anyway, just like I always do after something happens during a race weekend. Just like I will continue to do until the day he retires.

I'll support Leonard forever, but my heart might give out from panic sooner than I'd like.

His eyes find me as soon as I rip the door open, a loopy smile slipping onto his face. His eyes are barely open as he takes me in, lifting one of his hands to get me to close the distance between us.

"There you are," he says when I'm finally beside him, wrapping his hand in both of mine before bringing it to my chest. "My beautiful wife."

"You scared the shit out of me," I mumble, trying to keep my hands from shaking. A frown replaces his grin.

"I'm sorry, sweetheart. I tried not to faint, but I was so tired," he says, his head falling backward and onto the pillow. "I'm still so tired."

"I know, *amore*. You can rest now, I'm here. And when we get back, I'm calling the people in charge, and I'm ripping them to shreds. They should have called it off. They shouldn't have made you finish this race, any of you." Anger threatens to make my blood boil.

"It's fine, Starling, I'm fine. I should have trained harder than this. I should have—" I cut him off.

"No, Leonard, this isn't your fault. You *fainted*. They scheduled this race during the hottest time of the year, didn't listen to your and other drivers' radio messages, made you finish the race, and then *you fainted*. That isn't on you or any lack of training. No one should have to endure this," I say because there is no way in hell Leonard is going to blame himself for what happened.

"I *am* older than the others," he argues, so I squeeze the hand I'm holding and shake my head.

"Then why did Adrian tell me he threw up? Why did several of the other guys, too? Why did Rick come first but then saw black spots in his vision?" I settle down on his bed, placing a hand on his chest. "You're barely thirty-two, Leonard," I say. He studies my face, his eyelids fluttering shut, then slowly opening again.

"I don't want to be in the top team anymore, little demon. I don't want this pressure. I'm going to finish out my contract, but after next season, I want to switch to a smaller team. Two or three more years there, and then I want to retire," he replies, and I barely keep my lips from parting in surprise.

"Really? Why?" I ask, knowing full well he could race for another decade if he wanted.

"Because I want to be home more. Because I'm sick of being so far in the spotlight. I know I can't just stop. The world would hate me forever, more than a lot of them already do, and I don't want to disappoint those who've been rooting for me since the beginning. But I do want to stop racing. I want more time with you, to be with my family."

He sits up, even when I put my hands on his shoulders to get him to stop. He simply grabs my wrists and pulls one to his mouth, kissing it.

"Jack and Stu are thinking about adopting another child. Graham and Irena are getting married soon. Mum and Dad are getting older. Most importantly, whenever I'm away from you, I feel uneasy. I feel incomplete. I miss you so much." I know his feelings are even more heightened after that scare today, but the way he looks at me, the way he has always looked at me like I'm his entire world, tells me this is something he's thought about long before today's events.

"I miss you, too. When you're not home, my nights are cold. My days feel dragged out. I don't feel as excited to go home." He smiles at my words. "I support you through everything. You know that." Leonard nods, kissing my wrist again.

"I want to have a baby with you, sweetheart. I want to grow our family. Is that something you feel ready for, or would you like to wait a bit longer?"

Because, while it's a decision we make as a married couple, I get the final say. I get to decide when I'm ready, and I love him so much for never making me feel bad when I tell him I'm not ready. When I tell him I'm scared. When I tell him I don't even know if I want to carry our child or adopt them.

Before we got married, we spoke about having kids. Both of us wanted to, we just wanted to wait a few years. Recently, I've been thinking a lot about it. With me thriving in my dream job, which gives me the time and opportunity to have a kid, to be pregnant, I've thought a lot about what I'd like to do.

"If I can, I want to have our baby. I want to start trying," I tell him, a smile spreading over my lips when I see the happy expression covering his features.

"Yeah?" he asks, pushing off the pillow to get closer to me. Leonard grabs my face in his hands, his brown eyes now wide open.

"Yes," I reply, feeling his lips on mine a second later. He kisses me all over before hugging me to his chest, my ear resting right on top of his racing heart.

"Are you sure?" he asks as he pulls back, kissing my lips before I can answer his question.

"Very sure," I reply, smiling so hard my cheeks hurt. "But, for now, husband, you need sleep. Then we can make a baby," I say with a mischievous smirk that he returns.

"Oh, I'm looking forward to it, sweetheart."

CHAPTER 6
Leonard

"This is not what I had in mind when I said we should go relax at the beach," Jack says, his husband snickering behind him.

Stu's attention is dragged to Benz, who barks at another dog that walks by. It's her way of telling the other dog to play with her, and so is her tail wagging from side to side and her bowing down. When the other dog ignores her, she barks again, this time a little more irritated. I give her a pet on the head, then turn back to my niece.

"Come on, Lizzie. Your dad doesn't know what fun is," I say and hold out my hand for her. She's gotten so much taller, and I get sad every time I look at how grown she is now.

Lizzie lets out a small giggle before taking my hand and following me toward the jet ski I rented for today. There is one more beside the black one I took for myself, but Chiara is already on it, cocking a brow in challenge.

God, she looks devastatingly hot on that machine, with her thick thighs slung over the seat, her trained arms holding onto the grips. The bikini bottom she put on hugs her arse wonderfully, and I almost tripped over my own feet when she took her dress off and revealed the thin piece of fabric covering her breasts. They're hidden now underneath her lifejacket, and, fuck, I want to take it off her again so I can admire her chest.

"Uncle Lenny," Lizzie says, pulling at my life jacket to get my attention.

"Yeah, sorry, love. I'm paying attention," I say, helping her onto the jet ski before getting on myself.

"Can I tell you something, Uncle Lenny?" she asks once I've turned on the engine.

"Always," I reply, twisting my head to look at my niece. She's grinning now, wiggling in the seat as she directs her gaze toward my little demon.

"I think you have a crush on Chiara." I almost burst into laughter, a nostalgic feeling spreading through my chest.

"Can I tell you something, Lizzie?" I reply, and when she nods eagerly, I add, "No one has ever had a bigger crush on someone than I have on your Aunt Chiara."

"Yeah, your friend Adrian does. On himself." Surprise has me almost choking on my laughter.

"You've got a point," I say once I've stopped laughing long enough to reply.

"I saw him fix his hair three times once before smiling at himself in the mirror." Yeah, that sounds like Adrian. "But he's very attractive, so I guess it makes sense," she adds, her words barely more than a whisper. I turn my head to see a blush creeping onto her face.

"I think you may also have a crush," I point out, poking her side.

"Well, who doesn't have a crush on Adrian Romana?" the eleven-year-old challenges, and I shake my head with another laugh.

"Yeah, alright, you might be right."

Without another word, I start the engine. My brother yells for us to be careful, and I wave him off once before telling Lizzie to keep her arms around me.

She has so much fun, but I can see my brother getting impatient and worried, so I bring her back sooner than I think she'd like. Lizzie gets off the jet ski with a frown, but Jack wraps his arms around his daughter immediately. She rolls her eyes, turning her head my way to show me she's perfected the skill already.

"Hey, Champ, you coming?" Chiara calls out, tilting her head as she brings her jet ski to a stop next to me.

She turns back around, water spraying everywhere as she shoots forward and away from me. With a shake of my head and a smile covering my lips, I speed after my wife. She lifts her arse off the seat as she picks up the pace, and my mouth starts watering at the sight, my body humming with need.

Since I fainted after my race almost a week ago, Chiara's been a bit more on the "Leonard, you need rest" trip. On one hand, she's absolutely right. My entire body hurt up until yesterday. I could hardly move. On the other, we went from fucking almost every night to nothing in a week. It's all on me, and the way she looks over her shoulder and grins before wiggling her arse tells me she knows how horny I've been.

What she doesn't seem to consider is that she's just as horny, if not more than me. My insatiable little demon.

I catch up to her, leaning over a little to grab her right arse cheek. She grins at me before increasing her speed and putting more space between us. Waves shake the jet ski, making me bounce up and down as I chase after her, adrenaline coursing through my veins.

"Keep up, old man," she calls to me, our four-year age gap her weapon of choice for the third day in a row. She found it especially amusing when I kept making wheezing noises while bending down to retrieve my shoes because of how sore my body was.

"I have a proposal for you," I say when I'm close enough for her to hear me. She slows down until we're both stopped, swaying from side to side on our jet skis.

"What's your proposal, Champ?" I start circling her, revving the engine a little.

"You see those two boats over there?" I ask and nod toward the yachts that are facing each other, forming a finish line. Chiara nods, excitement sparkling in her eyes. "If you make it through there first, you choose where I take this bikini off. If I get through there first, we're going to our car and I'll rip it off in there, then slip deep inside of you," I say, watching the way her breathing picks up pace.

"The car is too far. Right here, bent over the jet ski, would be way more fun," she replies, and I almost choke on my next breath.

While that would be more fun, we're not exactly alone out here.

But I tell her, "Deal," anyway.

She shoots forward without warning, so I race after her. I increase my speed, more adrenaline coursing through me as I attempt to win this race against my wife. It's close, too, but I make it through the boats before her, a victorious, cheerful sound escaping me. I've never even made that sound after winning a race, but I've also never had this much fun.

"Fuck, I really wanted to see if you'd do it," she says with a mischievous smile.

We make our way back to the shore, and I waste no time throwing Chiara over my shoulder and carrying her toward our car.

"Where the bloody hell are you going?" Jack calls after us, making Chiara giggle.

"None of your business," I reply, slapping Chiara's arse cheek once when she lets out a louder laugh.

Once we're at the car, I open the backseat door, carefully lowering her onto the seat before joining her in there.

I've never been more grateful for tinted windows and for having parked in the shade about a mile away from the beach entrance.

"I wouldn't have done it," I say, pulling down the zipper of her life jacket. She takes it off without hesitation, throwing it in the trunk and facing me again. My hands move to cup her breasts, and she arches her back into my touch, letting me slide down her bikini top and rub my thumbs over her pebbled nipples.

"Why?" she asks, a moan escaping her.

"Because no one else gets to see you come, Chiara Tick. Only me."

CHAPTER 7
Chiara

It's the last race of the season.

Leonard and Rick are only two points apart.

My husband has been on edge for the past few days, getting nervous about how this season is going to end. He wants one last title. One more before he retires. If he can't get it this year, he still has next season to try again, but he's worked so hard to be on top, fighting Rick and Velocità Rossa every race weekend. He's put everything into being the fastest: stayed late with his team, trained harder than ever before, and tried out new adjustments to maximize the speed of the car.

He deserves the title.

It wouldn't just be handed to him.

It wouldn't be because he had no competition.

It would be because he had to fight hard for it.

"Sweetheart, I love you, but if you don't stop bouncing your legs, I might have to take a separate car," he says, dragging me out of my thoughts. I look down at my legs, watching them shake anxiously.

"Sorry," I mumble, using all of my strength to keep them from bouncing of their own volition. My hands cover my thighs, trying to hold them down.

Leonard's hand slides on top of mine, his fingers intertwining with mine.

"Is it because of what's at stake or because we're at another race with a high temperature?"

"Both," I admit without having to think about it. "I don't want you to be hospitalized again." Leonard chuckles, pulling my hand to his mouth to kiss my fingers. I watch him with my eyebrows pulled together because he seems a lot calmer now that he noticed I'm nervous. It doesn't make any sense.

"I'll be fine. I'll win the race today. I'll get that trophy. And everything will be fine." His promise doesn't soothe my nerves.

"Yeah, I know." But knowing and keeping from feeling a sense of dread in my stomach are two very different things.

"And, if I don't, you're not allowed to divorce me." I almost burst into laughter at how ridiculous he sounds.

"But I only married you because I thought you'd win *three* championships, not *two*," I tease back, so Leonard squeezes my inner thigh, making me squeal in my seat. "I'm kidding. I obviously only married you for your money." Leonard bursts into laughter, a sound reserved for me and me alone.

"And I didn't even make you sign a prenup." He shakes his head.

"*I* didn't make *you* sign one either, and I'm a very successful business owner," I remind him, even if he needs no reminder.

Leonard has this habit of telling everyone we meet about my accomplishments before he even speaks of his own. Just last week, he told a woman we met at a *driver event* about *Meteorite* and the exhibits she can find there. He even gave her the location of the gallery so she could go there when she's in London next time.

"I am a very lucky man indeed," he says, leaning over when we're stopped at the red light to kiss my cheek.

Benz and I go to Leonard's garage while he meets up with Quinn and his race engineer. Robert Fuchs, the team principal of Grenzenlos, greets me with a warm smile. He hands me a pair of headphones before offering me kind, reassuring words that do nothing to ease the ache in my chest. I felt the same way when Leonard was this close to his second championship. I wanted to throw up, bite my nails, scream. Anything to relieve this tension in my chest.

"The car is fast. Leonard is starting from pole position. The Velocità Rossa drivers have been struggling with oversteering and brake overheating all weekend. The odds are in our favor," he assures me, but I know the odds can change very quickly in Formula One.

I've watched it long enough, been a fan for as long, and have seen how easily a driver who looks confident and comfortable can end up in the wall. Whether it's another driver or something going wrong with the car, in Formula One, you have to learn to expect the unexpected. It's too inconsistent sometimes to believe it's anything less than unpredictable.

All I offer Robert Fuchs is my usual scowl and a curt nod.

Allie from Leonard's team takes Benz to a separate room while I make my way to the screens. I'm nervous all over again. Another member approaches me with a coffee, but I shake my head. If I have caffeine right now, I might bounce off the walls.

"Relax, he's ready," Quinn tells me once she joins me in the garage. "He's focused, in his bubble. He's got this." It's as much of a reassurance for me as it is for herself.

"Days like these take at least five years off my lifespan," I say, pinching the front of my Grenzenlos shirt to push and pull quickly, making a bit of wind hit my sweaty face. Quinn laughs, then nods in agreement.

"Why do you think I have so many wrinkles even though I'm only in my thirties?" she asks, grabbing my hand to give it a comforting squeeze. "All he has to do is bring it home."

"Yeah, you're right. Leonard will be fine," I say, squeezing her hand back.

Soon, the drivers take their formation lap. More beads of nervous sweat roll down my neck and back. Leonard drives his car back to the first place on the grid, making my breathing hitch when he has to break a bit harder to keep his tire from moving over the line. It's a rookie mistake, which is probably why Quinn grabs my arm as she watches the screens in front of us.

"Maybe he's nervous, after all," she says to herself, so quietly I barely hear her over the loud noises in the garage and the headphones covering my ears.

I wish I hadn't heard it because that uncomfortable feeling constricting my chest multiplies by a million. My breaths are so shallow that I feel dizzy. I inhale deeply, then hold before exhaling again. I do that until my heart slows a little.

I used to do this before every one of my fights, especially the ones I thought I'd lose.

But Leonard isn't losing today.

He'll win.

I believe in him.

The lights above the drivers flash on one by one until every single red dot fills the bottom row of the starting light system.

One.

Two.

Three.

Four.

Five.

I hold my breath, my fingers flying to my mouth as I press my lips shut.

The urge to go hide in the room Benzie is in and ignore what's happening on the screen is strong, but I manage to keep my eyes open to watch all the lights disappear.

Leonard has a fantastic start and stays ahead of Rick and Jonathan. But the Velocitá Rossa driver is right behind my husband, trying to find the slipstream to overtake him.

The first two laps pass slowly, and my focus is on the gap between Rick and Leonard. For the first few laps, DRS is disabled, but as they cross the line for the third time, Rick is less than a second behind Champ, and his DRS flap opens.

He shoots past Leonard.

"*Cazo!*" I yell at the screen, everyone near me in the garage turning their heads to look at me. One of the mechanics, Ben, who never really liked me, places a finger over his lips to tell me to shut up. So, I add, "*Vaffanculo,*" and throw my middle finger up in his direction. Quinn smacks my hand away, but she's laughing so hard, I'm convinced she's crying a little.

When I look back at the screen, I watch Leonard take back the first-place position.

His car is ahead of Rick's when all of a sudden, time stops.

The red Velocità Rossa's front wing touches my husband's Grenzenlos' tire, puncturing it. It explodes, the rubber flying off before sparks fill the air from where the rim meets the ground. Then, Leonard's car spins right into Rick's, sending them both off the track and into the barriers.

My heart drops into my stomach.

The entire scene plays out almost as if in slow motion, dragging out this nightmare of a moment.

I don't mean to, but I sink into a squat, my hand covering my mouth to hide the way my jaw has dropped. While Leonard has forbidden the media from filming the section of the garage where I'm standing after the death threats and hate messages I received, I can never be too sure that they stick to the agreement, especially in knee-weakening, agonizing moments like these.

Leonard's chance to win the championship, get his third title, his last goal in this sport at this point in his life, is gone. Vanished like he didn't work an entire season to get here. Disappeared while Rick, who caused the fucking accident, is now World Champion.

My eyes lift back to the screens, taking in the way Leonard stays in his car for a long moment, hitting his wheel over and over in pain. His radio message fills my ears, the sound of his scream making tears shoot into my eyes.

"Fuck," Quinn says, her hand slipping onto my shoulder as she kneels beside me. "Come on, Chiara, you should go to his private room. He'll need you when he gets back," she says, but I haven't regained the feeling in my legs yet.

"Everything he worked for this year is just gone, all in the blink of an eye," I say, fighting back the tears when the sound of Leonard's scream replays in my ears.

Why the fuck do they have to replay that?

I rip the headphones off and hand them to Quinn, staring at the screen one last time to see Leonard jump out of the car and make his way toward the marshals waiting for him. They guide him through an opening in the track fencing, letting him climb on the back of one of the mopeds to drive him back to his garage. Rick does the same with a different marshal driving him.

Seeing Leonard leave his car behind, officially out of the race, snaps me out of my trance. I walk toward his private room, ready to break several pieces of the furniture in here to let out my frustration.

Instead, I take a deep breath and hop onto the table where Leonard gets massaged. My fingers wrap around the edge while I drop my head and swing my legs, waiting impatiently.

A long time after the crash, my husband steps into the room, his balaclava and helmet hanging from his hand.

"I lost," he says, tears stinging his eyes. "I didn't get the third title."

"I know, *amore*." He drops the helmet and balaclava before rushing toward me. His arms wrap around me, his hand cupping the back of my head as he holds me close. "I'm so sorry," I say, hugging him back. His scent combined with sweat fills my nose, my hands feeling the wet fabric of his fireproofs at his back.

"I failed," he adds, pulling back to let me see his handsome features have pulled into a sad expression. I raise my fingers to his lips, tracing the frown painted on them.

"You didn't fail. That crash was not on you, Leonard." He kisses me as soon as the words have left my mouth, but it's swift, only a brush of our lips before he hugs me again.

"But I still lost. Rick is World Champion."

There is nothing I can say that will cheer him up. Nothing that can ease the sense of failure or the pain in his chest.

All I can do is hold onto him.

So, I do.

I bring my legs around his waist and dig my heels into his butt to bring him closer. With his chest flush against mine, he chuckles into my ear, pulling back enough to bring his lips back onto mine. He kisses me long and deep, seeking comfort in the taste of me. I part my lips, feeling his tongue slip into my mouth, exploring me.

He takes his time, only pulling back when both of us are out of breath, my cheeks probably flushed. I'm a little turned on, like always, and I love the way he smiles at me because he knows what a simple kiss from him does to me.

But then he remembers what just happened, and he frowns all over again.

"You have one more season, Champ. You wanted one more championship, and you have one last chance. You will get your third title, and you will leave Grenzenlos on a fucking high, you hear me?" I ask, earning a smile from my husband.

"I hear you, wife. And you're right," he replies, kissing the tip of my nose, his warm brown eyes on me.

"I usually am." The smug smile that follows is entirely out of my control.

"You usually are," he agrees, leaning down to press his forehead to mine. "One last chance." I nod in agreement.

"For one last championship."

Chapter 8
Leonard

I've been looking forward to today for the past few weeks. After the disappointing last race of the season, where Rick crashed into me and secured himself as World Champion, I've been struggling to enjoy anything that isn't related to Chiara. I love being with her, but I can't spend my entire winter break at *Meteorite* just so I can watch her work. I'm a distraction, especially because I keep dragging her to her office, placing her on the desk, and losing myself in her.

At one point, Chiara even threatened to ban me from the art gallery for distracting her. She laughed like it was a funny joke, but I was temporarily scared shitless.

We're still trying to get pregnant, but so far, the two pregnancy tests my little demon took came back negative. But I'm most certainly still enjoying trying over and over.

I don't think that will ever get boring if I'm being honest.

"Remind me how you know MotoGP World Champion Julián Alvarez again," Chiara whispers as we make our way out of the car and toward the track where Julián "Storm" Alvarez, Adrian, and I will be racing some 1000cc Hawke MotoGP motorcycles. Julián rides for Hawke, so he invited me to race a few months ago. When I told Adrian, he practically dropped to his knees, begging me to let him come.

"Julián reached out to me a few years ago, asking if I could talk to Robert Fuchs and see if he has an internship position open for his girlfriend. My team turned her away and so did Alfa Adrenalina, so she became a championship-winning race engineer for her husband's team," I explain, watching Starling nod several times as she processes that piece of information. I'm about to smile at her when I spot a mop of blonde curls in my peripheral.

"Well, oh well, if it isn't my 'the one that got away,'" Adrian teases, earning an eye roll from my wife and a hint of a smile. I, on the other hand, grab my good friend by the collar of his polo shirt and drag him away from Starling.

"Eyes off my wife, playboy," I warn, but the wanker throws a smirk over his shoulder at Chiara anyway. I slap him up the back of his head, making him curse under his breath.

"Alright, God, what crawled up your ass today?" he asks, rubbing his head where I slapped him.

"You did when you started flirting with Chiara," I reply and scowl at him, but he merely furrows his brows at me.

"I only do that because she always almost smiles when I flirt with her. I amuse her. I love bringing people joy and, while the two of you may not show it as outwardly as others, I know I can entertain you both this way," he explains, but he doesn't have to.

Bringing people he cares about happiness, even if it is merely through eliciting a smile from them, makes Adrian happy. He's like the class clown of the Formula One world. Even though he has some of the darkest demons. I know he pretends they don't exist, hides his grief in compartments in his head and locks them away, but they're there. They haunt him when he's not careful about keeping them hidden away, and I wish he'd let me in.

While I may not understand his pain, I'd be there for him no matter what.

Neither one of us speaks again. I look over my shoulder, holding out my hand for Chiara when I notice she's fallen behind a little. I don't move another centimetre, not until her fingers lace through mine.

Adrian walks ahead of us, smiling at everyone we pass. I watch him with disbelief, especially because of the way everyone returns his sunshine smile as if they're compelled to do so.

I almost welcome the way Julián Alvarez scowls at the bike in front of him, then at the person beside him. From what I've gathered, he's as much of a grump as Chiara and me, and I love it. I'm constantly surrounded by people who cannot stop smiling—Cameron, Adrian, Quinn—sometimes it feels like Chiara and I are storm clouds in an otherwise sunny world.

But Julián is living, frowning proof that we're not.

Then, my eyes drift to Scarlette, his wife, and I almost groan. Her face is practically a ray of sunshine, blinding everyone with her joy.

"What do these people have to be so happy about?" Chiara grumbles next to me, so I warp my arm around her shoulders and pull her against my side, my lips connecting with her temple.

"I love you so much," I say before kissing her head again and chuckling against her skin.

After everyone greeted each other, Scarlette giving me that same star-struck look she wore when we first met years ago, Julián leads Adrian and me to a blue and black bike as well as an orange and black one.

"How well-versed are the two of you with motorbikes?" the MotoGP champion asks, crossing his arms in front of his chest as he faces us.

"I've been taking riding lessons since I found out we were doing this," Adrian says, so proud of himself that he puffs out his chest a little.

I almost feel bad for stealing the spotlight from him with my next sentence.

"I used to ride motorcycles when I was younger, but I stopped when I turned twenty-five because my team told me it's too dangerous," I explain, watching Adrian's head whip my way, his jaw dropping.

"Fuck off! Is there anything you can't do?" he asks, slapping my arm with the back of his hand, an impressed look crossing his face.

"Get rid of you, apparently," I reply, making Adrian burst into laughter.

"That's right, you're stuck with me. *Muhahahahaha*." Adrian's evil laugh turns into a fit of laughter. Julián watches him with an unimpressed quirk of his brow, then shifts his gaze to me and shakes his head in disbelief.

"Is *rubio* always this giggly?" he asks, making me tilt my head at the Spanish word.

"*Rubio*?" Julián shrugs.

"It means 'blondie,'" he explains, which is quite fitting for the man who still hasn't recovered from laughing.

"Yeah, he's always like this. You get used to it," I assure him.

"I'm not sure I want to," Julián replies, but when Adrian straightens out his back and his laughter immediately dies out, the motorcycle racer almost smiles.

"I haven't met a single person who could resist my charm, Storm. You won't be the first," Adrian says, smirking down at Julián.

"I've always enjoyed being the first at something. It's why I've been MotoGP champion for two years in a row," the Puerto Rican says before throwing the Monegasque a wink.

Adrian's jaw drops again, both of us watching Julián walk away to grab our gear.

"I don't know if I'm pissed or a little turned on," he blurts out, but I merely shrug.

"Once you understand that you can be both at the same time, then you'll also understand Chiara's and my relationship."

That makes him throw me a wolfish grin.

"Come on, you two. I haven't got all day," Julián says, and Adrian gives my arm a nudge to get me to move.

"Let's go. I've gotta make this man like me somehow," Adrian whispers to me, both of us making our way over to the grumpy racer.

"You know he's married, right?" I tease.

"And while I may look like I wouldn't hurt a fly, I'll fight anyone who makes a move on my husband," Scarlette Roots-Alvarez chimes in, throwing us a bright smile.

"Don't worry, beautiful, I'd never get between a husband and a wife, unless they invite me to join them," Adrian replies, directing his smirk at her instead.

"Do you have an off button?" I ask, tugging on my shirt when I see Julián holding out racing leathers.

"Nope. I'm always turned on." I wish I would have filmed the way his face went from all smug to blushing from embarrassment. Scar giggles to herself. "That's not what I meant," he adds with a breathless, humorless laugh. "Fuck, I can't recover from that. Let's just pretend this didn't happen." If I were a nicer friend, maybe I would.

"I'll never let you live this down," I chime in, and Adrian slaps his forehead with the palm of his hand. I can't help but smile a little, but when he looks at me, I go back to scowling.

I have a reputation to uphold, after all.

Once we've all changed into our racing suits, Julián and I return to the garage where the bikes are. Chiara and Scarlette are deep in conversation, but when Scarlette sees her husband approach her with the front of his suit still open to expose his trained chest, she blushes immediately. She reaches for his zipper, slowly dragging it up while keeping eye contact. His eyes are heated with desire. As soon as his suit is zipped up, he captures her lips with his. Scarlette laughs against his mouth, her hands slipping into his hair.

I turn toward my wife, noticing the way her eyes are raking over my body. Half her bottom lip slips between her teeth as she admires me. I close the distance between us, grabbing her hips, pulling her against me, and kissing her.

"How badly do you want to rip this suit off me right now?" I mumble against her mouth before kissing her again.

"Very badly. Is that an option?" she replies when I kiss down her neck. My arms wrap around her torso, lifting her onto her tiptoes to hug her to my chest.

"Later," I promise, pressing my lips to Chiara's one more time. "Definitely later," I add when her gaze drops down to my bulge again. So insatiable. It makes my heart skip a beat every single time.

"I think this suit might be a bit too small," Adrian announces as he reappears in the garage with the suit hanging at his waist, his chest completely exposed. Standing there half-naked and looking more confident than anyone has a right to, he points at his abs. "Don't think this is very safe."

Chiara and Scarlette both stare at Adrian's bare chest for a moment, studying every ridge and ripple carved out of muscle. I place a hand over Chiara's eyes a second later, fighting back a displeased groan.

"Zip up your suit," I say through gritted teeth, but Adrian throws his hands up in frustration.

"I tried, but I'm too tall and wide," he explains, attempting to pull the suit up but failing.

"Here, I think I have a bigger size," Scarlette says with a snicker, throwing the suit at the Monegasque's head. He catches it with ease, throwing her a smile before disappearing again.

Meanwhile, Julián shows me everything I need to know about the bike before giving Adrian the same explanation when he rejoins us. I put on the balaclava and helmet, feeling the padding of the racing suit to make sure that in case anything happens, I'm protected. The season is going to start in two weeks, so I can't injure myself now. If my team even knew I was doing this, they'd chain me to the nearest pillar to stop me.

It's why I didn't tell them.

"You both feel ready?" Julián asks after he finishes giving us a crash course. He's also wearing his helmet now, and so is Adrian.

"Yes, sir," my friend replies, saluting the MotoGP racer as if he's our commanding officer.

Julián merely shakes his head, turning around without another word. Adrian's hand drops next to his body, his shoulders sagging in defeat.

"Well, the day has finally come. I've lost my charm," he says before spinning my way and dropping his helmeted head against my shoulder. Fake crying sounds, muffled through the padding, come from him, so I smack the backside of his helmet.

"Get a grip, mate. One person not liking you isn't the end of the world," I say, but Adrian merely bangs his head against mine.

"Maybe not for you," he replies, stepping toward his bike and flinging his leg over it.

Julián's team instructs us to wait another moment before giving us the "Go" signal. Julián is the first one to drive out of the pits, but Adrian and I follow closely behind.

Adrenaline sweeps through me as we speed down the track, leaning into the corners. Julián, like the professional he is, goes lower than us, but neither Adrian nor I are ready to follow his lead yet.

But that's precisely why we race more than one lap.

CHAPTER 9

Chiara

"I'll never get tired of watching Julián race," Scarlette says, turning to offer me a bright, warm smile. Her blue eyes sparkle with joy.

"I have to admit, this is extremely attractive," I reply and point at the screen where Leonard leans into the corner, trying out a lower position for the first time since they went out to race. "Maybe I should convince Leonard to get another bike," I blurt out, finding Scarlette's presence strangely comfortable.

"Oh, do it. Matter of fact, get your own license and ride with him. My husband and I go on riding dates at least once a week," she replies, nudging me with her shoulder like we're old friends. And damn, it does feel that way.

"Only once a week?" I tease, but Scarlette's expression turns mischievous.

"We've tried going twice in a week once but... well, we never made it out of our garage, if you know what I mean." A blush creeps up her neck and settles on her cheeks.

"Oh yeah, I know what you mean. Leonard and I would be very similar in that way." If we even made it once a week.

"It's still fun though. As long as you're safe, that is. Julián's best friend, Elias, got into a nasty crash a year ago. Scared all of us. It was a combination of reckless driving from another driver and Elias' lack of wearing proper safety gear. A helmet isn't enough," she explains, and I nod along to her words, watching a serious look take over her soft features.

"Is he okay now?" I ask, feeling a bit of concern for someone I've never even met.

"Yeah, he's fine. He's got a heck of a scar though." *Heck?*

Before I can fight my smile at the way Scarlette apparently doesn't curse, I notice all three racers take a corner together. Adrian and Leonard are behind Julián, but only barely. As soon as they get back on a straight, my husband and Adrian pick up their speed, chasing the MotoGP World Champion.

"Tell me they're not actually racing," I blurt out, taking a step toward the screens without meaning to. My heart stumbles all over itself as Leonard leans forward on the bike, going even faster.

"I think they are," Scarlette replies and chuckles at the two idiots I've grown to love trying to catch her husband.

When Julián turns his head to see what Leonard and Adrian are trying to do, he increases his speed and disappears down the straight, leaving them far behind. He makes his way down the track and back over the finish line long before the other two. I shake my head right as Leonard and Adrian cross it too, Scarlette snickering to herself like this is the funniest thing she's watched in a long time.

And it is, at least to me.

All three men make their way back to the pits two laps later, revving their engines so loudly, I hear the bikes long before I see them.

Julián is the first to park his machine and hop off, making his way over to Scarlette.

"Don't you dare," she says, but he wraps his arms around her anyway, probably completely drenched in sweat. "Julián!" she squeals, and I look away when his hands slip lower and lower down her back.

A moment later, a sweaty body presses against me, Leonard's lips finding mine. He didn't even take off his balaclava, merely pulled it down so he could kiss me, his tongue swiping over my bottom lip. I part my lips, feeling it slip into my mouth.

There's something very special about the way Leonard kisses me when he's still high on the adrenaline rush. It's different from other times he kisses me. His mouth on mine is always a heady feeling, but it's even more so when his emotions are running high. It's like he transfers them onto me, letting me share in everything he feels.

I also love that I'm always the first person he rushes to, the first person he wants to touch when he feels invincible. I'm not a racer, but he lets me in on the thrill of it to the best of his ability. He lets me feel his racing heart as it pounds between our chests. He lets me feel his excitement as it vibrates off him and onto my skin, leaving goosebumps in its wake. He lets me in on how much he loves the sport, even when he thinks he's lost his passion for it somewhere along the way.

It's easy to lose myself in the kiss. I love to sink completely into it until the rest of the world vanishes, but there are people around, so I do my best to keep from sliding my hands onto his nape. From pulling him closer until I feel every ridge, every muscle pressed against me.

I love my husband's body.

I love my husband's heart and soul even more.

"That was exhilarating," he whispers against my mouth, kissing me one more time, long and deep, before stepping back.

"It sure was," I say, a little weak in the knees. Noticing the way I sway on my feet, Leonard grabs hold of my forearms, steadying me.

"You okay, sweetheart?"

"More than," I say, smiling up at him while he smirks down at me.

"I feel like a fifth wheel," Adrian says, pulling me out of my trance.

"Well, if you weren't so anti-relationship, you could have a partner to kiss right now," Leonard replies, looking over his shoulder at his friend.

"I'd rather be a fifth wheel, thanks," he adds with a scoff, shuddering at the very thought of giving himself over to someone else.

Instead of weighing in and telling Adrian that I know he's capable of loving someone more fiercely than any of us could ever begin to imagine, I run a hand down Leonard's chest. My husband turns his head my way, cocking an intrigued brow at me.

"What do you want, Starling?" he says, quiet enough to ensure I'm the only one who hears him.

"To go back to our hotel and rip this off you," I whisper back, my hand dropping even lower.

Leonard catches my wrist, stopping me from going any further.

"Anything my wife wants, she gets."

CHAPTER 10
Leonard

"He's absolutely adorable," Chiara says, bouncing on her heel to soothe the crying baby. "Hi, baby boy," she coos, her gaze softer than I've ever seen it before. Hearing her baby voice, Benz runs up to her Mamma, nudging her leg with her nose, desperate for attention.

I take in the image in front of me for a moment longer, snapping a mental picture of it and storing it away in my "perfect memories" folder.

"I'm so happy for you," I tell Jack and Stu, who've been watching the newest addition of their little family with tears in their eyes ever since we came here today.

Mum and Dad have been patiently waiting to hold their grandchild again, but Chiara hasn't let go of the little guy since Jack handed him to her. Bouncing on her feet, she keeps talking to the baby. Jack and Stu haven't decided on a name yet. He's only been with them for less than a day, but my brothers said they'll wait however long is necessary, until they know for sure what name belongs to their son. The three-month-old will just have to wait until the two most indecisive people make up their minds.

"I think I'll keep you, sweet boy," Chiara says, chuckling when Jack lets out a shocked gasp.

"I will hunt you to the ends of the bloody Earth, Chiara de Luca," my brother says, so I shoot him a glare.

"*Tick*. Her last name is Tick," I correct him, earning an amused grin from my wife.

"God, so possessive." Stu's smile is mean, but I simply roll my eyes and focus on Starling again, enjoying the way she looks at the bundle in her arms.

She seems so happy. Like she can't wait to finally hold our own baby.

"Chiara, may I hold my grandbaby now?" Mum chimes in, and, very reluctantly, my little demon hands her the baby. A single tear spills down my mother's face as she traces her grandson's cheek, nose, and forehead. "I wish I could see you, my little treasure."

More tears fall from Mum's eyes, and I'm about to step toward her, describe what he looks like, when Chiara beats me to it.

She squats down beside Mum's chair, putting one hand on her arm and one on top of the baby's head.

"He's beautiful," she starts. "He has dark skin, a small but wide nose, brown eyes, and right now, a crinkle between his brow as he looks at the blue sky."

Mum wasn't born blind. She lost her vision when she was in her mid-forties because of retinitis pigmentosa, an eye disease that attacks retinas. It happened gradually, losing more and more of her sight over time. Most days, she says she's accepted it. If you ask me, she's absolutely incredible for how she adapted to one of her senses being taken away from her. But on days like today, she suffers a lot. She got to see everyone in our family before she lost her vision, but not her grandbabies.

"Thank you," Mum says, one of her hands searching for Chiara's face to cup her cheek. I notice tears glistening in Starling's eyes, but she swallows them down as her hand reaches up to cover Mum's.

"Anytime, Mum."

Something stitches itself back together inside of me at that single word. Mum has always seen Chiara as her child. Ever since we were kids, Chiara has been part of our family. She didn't live with us, but she spent so much time around Graham and my parents, she became an honorary Tick for them.

But I was stupid. I avoided her like she was a DNF because every time I saw her, we fought.

Until I couldn't stay away anymore.

Until her well-being and happiness started to outrank the rest of the world.

Until I realised she was all I wanted.

And now she's my family. By name and by heart, mind, and soul.

As soon as Chiara is standing again, I close the distance between us and place my hands on her hips to drag her against me. A gasp *whooshes* out of her, but when I spin her around, I notice the way her brow is cocked in amusement.

"Can't get enough of me, can you, Champ?" she asks, placing her hands on my cheeks as I step backward to let Jack, Stu, Graham, Irena, and Dad huddle around Mum to look at the baby.

"I'll never get enough of you, Chiara." My lips hit hers even as we continue walking backward, slipping into the house with Benz following closely behind.

"Where are you taking me?" she says, giggling as I lift her into my arms, her legs wrapping around my waist.

"My old bedroom. There's something that I want to show you," I explain, my hands dropping to her arse to cup it and squeeze.

"If it's your cock, I hate to break it to you, but I know every. Single. Centimetre." With every word, she brings her mouth toward mine, lowering her voice until seduction drips from it. "Intimately," she adds in a whisper, the tip of her tongue running over my bottom lip before she slips it into my mouth.

My body hums with pleasure and need, but I push past that feeling, breaking the kiss only long enough to say, "It's not my cock. Unless you want to drop to your knees and study it again." I love the way her cheeks turn pink from my words.

"What is it you want to show me?" she asks, nudging my nose with hers.

"Something of great value to me." She chuckles.

"I've already looked in the mirror today, Leonard." I can't help it. I burst into laughter, smacking her right arse cheek before nuzzling my face into her neck.

"You're impossible," I reply, putting her down right before we climb the stairs.

As she makes her way upstairs, swaying her arse from side to side, I barely contain the urge to touch it again.

Make her squeal.

Or moan.

Either would work for me.

Benz is still following us, wagging her tail as she struts right into my childhood bedroom. She sniffs the bed frame, carpet, and trophy shelf before sprinting out of the room again, leaving Chiara and me alone. I watch it all with fascination, but when Starling drops on the bed, her gaze tracing my shape, I grin. I shake my head at my insatiable little demon, but she merely shrugs.

"You brought me into a bedroom. You can only blame yourself," she says, reading my thoughts.

"While you may be right, can you focus for a few minutes before I give you what you want?" I ask, but my tone sounds more like I'm asking for permission than intended. I guess being married to Chiara has turned me more into a submissive man than I ever thought I would be.

"Fine," she says with a naughty smile, leaning back on the bed to watch me while I rummage around my room. "How come the only time I've ever been in your room is when Mum had her accident?" Chiara asks, her back flat on the mattress while she lifts one of my tyre-shaped plush toys into the air. Dad got it for me when I'd just turned six.

"Because we hated each other, remember?" Chiara snorts, and I chuckle. My fingers roam through the many photo albums and documents in a drawer at my desk. "Aha!" I say as I find what I've been looking for at the very bottom, pulling it out without any grace or subtlety. Chiara laughs as a bunch of documents spill onto the ground.

"Need some help there, Champ?" I frown at her, which only makes her laugh a little. "Two-time Formula One World Champion Leonard Tick can't pull a folder from a drawer without making a huge mess." I straighten out my back, scowling at her for teasing me.

"You think you're so funny."

"Just show me what you wanted to show me," she says, glaring at me until I smile at her, which always makes her features soften.

She loves my smile.

I love giving it to her.

I settle down on the bed beside her, pulling her legs onto my lap. Chiara's arms wrap around one of mine, her temple pressed against my shoulder. I place the scrapbook on her legs, the title "Leonard's Racing Accomplishments" written in my dad's handwriting.

"What is this?" she asks, her voice soft and full of awe. Her fingers trace the worn leather, the different materials—newspaper, cardboard, normal paper, and so on—catching her attention.

"It's what I want to do for our kids when the time comes. Should he, she, or they decide they want to go into racing." I open the book, revealing the first page.

The drawing of a trophy, kart, and pictures of me along with writing is displayed on the page. My father worked hours on this after I won my first karting race. After I told him racing was what I wanted to do for the rest of my life.

Back then, he spent every weekend I wasn't racing going to get the photos printed and then making new pages in the book. He'd encourage me to help, to use my creative side and add my touch to it. It's easy to spot exactly what I did because the difference between Dad's meticulous and thought-through work is incomparably better than the mess my six-year-old self scribbled and glued onto the page.

And yet, Chiara traces only what I added with her fingers. Studies my work closer than Dad's. As if she knows I'm the one who did it.

"No matter what our kids do, I want something like this for them. Do you think we can ask Dad to help us?" she asks, looking up at me with those beautiful green eyes of hers. Without thinking, I lean down to press my lips to hers.

"I'd love that."

We spent a little longer looking through the scrapbook, going over the pages of my first karting championship title and my F4 acceptance letter glued to one of the pages. We look through every page until we reach the end. The second to last one my dad made.

Tears fill my eyes at the sight of me holding the trophy of the last race of my first F1 championship-winning year. I've never seen this page before, most likely because it's so recent. Dad must have put it in here without me knowing, and I almost ball up and cry my eyes out at this very sweet gesture because it makes me feel like a kid all over again.

When I turn to the last page to see my second championship-winning year, one tear slips down my cheek. Chiara catches it, hugging my arm tighter. He left some space at the bottom of the page, the words "Leonard's Third Championship" written on top of the empty space.

"He believes in you." Starling's words catch my attention.

Until this very second, I had no idea how much I needed this. After the disappointment of last season and my lack of being able to do anything about the driver academy I've dreamt about for years now, I needed this more than I could have ever known.

"He knows you can do anything you put your mind to, *amore mio*. The academy. The championship. Any other dreams. Anything you want." She places her chin on my shoulder to study me, so I turn my head to look at her, letting her see the vulnerability in my eyes.

"Sometimes, it doesn't feel that way. Sometimes, all my accomplishments mean nothing to my mind. I doubt myself. I think I'm worthless. After what happened a few months ago, I feel like that even more so." I pause to suck in a sharp breath. "The media have made me feel this way my whole life, and I thought I was over it, but I don't think I am. The way they've been dragging me through the fucking mud, it's—" I break off, not finding the right word.

"Demotivating. Depreciating. Disgusting," she says, the last word making me smile. Hard.

"Yeah," is all I manage to say, my beautiful wife cupping my cheek as her enchanting eyes stay on mine.

"You're nothing like what they say you are. Those people can burn in hell because they have always taken any chance to shit on who you are when you are the best person I've ever met. I ever will meet. Your heart, Leonard, it's so, so big. So full of love. You give your all without ever expecting anything in return, and they don't see that. They never have. They see what they want to see, never deeper than the surface. That's the media's problem. And all the people that listen? They're just fucking sheep that can't think for themselves or haven't been educated well enough to form their own opinions about people. I know you know that. I know it's something you've had to deal with your entire life, but I want to remind you that they don't matter. None of their opinions do. But you know whose opinion matters?" she asks, and I smile at her, knowing where she's going with this.

"Yours," I reply, making her nod.

"Damn straight. Mine does. The opinions of those wonderful people sitting with our new nephew downstairs do. Adrian's does, but only because he holds you in such high regard that it's safe to put him on this list." The way she always finds a way to make me laugh will never not be astonishing to me. "Yours does, baby. But no one else's. Okay?" she asks, rubbing her thumb along my cheekbone. My eyes flutter shut at her touch.

"Okay," I mumble, my voice barely more than a whisper.

"I'm so proud of you," she says, unraveling me, only to put me back together with a single kiss.

They say you should marry your best friend. The person who knows you better than you even know yourself.

Chiara has always been so much more than a best friend. She's seen me at my worst, at my meanest. She's also seen me at my best, my kindest. We grew so close, always a touch away from becoming more. And I fell in love with her for so many reasons. Because she was my best friend. Because she was everything I could have ever wanted. Because she fit into my life so perfectly. Because she thinks my heart is big, but hers is even bigger. Because she's my soulmate.

So, in a way, I guess I did marry my best friend.

But I also married my soul's other half.

My life's purpose.

The reason I breathe.

"You're the best part of me, Chiara Tick."

"And you're the best part of me," she replies, leaning back to grin at me.

When we rejoin our family downstairs, I walk straight toward Dad, wrapping my arms around him without hesitation. He lets out an *oof* at the impact of my hug, but his arms find their way around me a moment later, his chuckle vibrating off him.

"You okay, son?" he asks, so I hold on tighter.

"Thank you. For everything. For being the best dad anyone could have ever asked for," I say, swallowing down my overwhelming emotions before they can spill down my cheeks.

"It's easy to be the best dad when you've got the best sons," he replies, nodding over at Graham, Jack, and Stu. Someone clears their throat behind us, and I let go of Dad to see my feisty wife with her hands on her hips and her eyebrows raised. "And daughter," Dad corrects, making a tiny smile tug at Chiara's mouth. "Come here," he adds, so my wife runs into his arms, too.

"I'm your only one, so I should get special treatment," she teases, making Dad burst into laughter.

"Hey, I gave you a husband and a best friend. What more do you want from me?" he asks.

Our whole family bursts into laughter, but Mum frowns at Dad's statement.

"You gave nothing, only a few seconds worth of something. *I* gave her them," she says, and Stu laughs so hard, tears shoot out of his eyes. My jaw drops as I stare at my mum, too surprised at her rebuttal to catch my jaw.

Chiara closes my mouth for me, and I mumble a quick, "Thank you, sweetheart," before turning to Dad to see his jaw has also dropped.

I burst into laughter, joining my entire family in their amusement and joy.

Chapter II

Chiara

Leonard has been stressed about the driver academy he's trying to open for the past three days, not even taking a break to eat unless I place a plate in front of him. I told him to come to work with me today so that I could keep an eye on him.

He calls me stubborn, but he's the more stubborn one out of the two of us when he sets his mind to something.

It's why his ring is on my finger.

"This exhibit is absolutely beautiful. We have to come again," I overhear a woman tell her girlfriend before pressing the sweetest kiss to her lips and walking out of my gallery.

Benz nudges my leg as my heart flutters from happiness, so I tear my eyes from the sight of the couple leaving and turn to my daughter. She nudges my leg again and whines at the same time I hear Leonard cursing from my office.

"Uh oh, should we check on your angry daddy before he rips my office to shreds?" I ask, and she runs in that direction as soon as the word "daddy" leaves my mouth. "Can you take over for a moment?" I ask Nari, my best employee, and she gives me a bright smile and quick nod. "Thank you."

I walk toward my office, worry settling in my chest when I hear him curse again. Benz paws at the door, so I open it for her, both of us stepping inside to see Leonard's face buried between his hands. A groan of frustration slips out of him as he rubs his palms over his eyes and then opens them again to look at me.

His beautiful brown eyes soften at the sight of Benz and me approaching, but I can tell whatever has him frustrated can't be fixed just because we're here.

"Do you want to tell me what's wrong?" I ask right as he pushes the chair away from the desk. He holds out both his hands to signal for me to join him.

Once I'm in front of him, sliding my hands into his, he guides me between his legs. Still not close enough, his fingers slip onto my hips, lifting me onto his lap. Leonard places his head on my chest, his ear pressed against where my heart is beating. His hair is short again, so I run my hands over it, playing with his curls.

"Talk to me," I say as he trails his fingers down my spine, over my ass, along my thighs.

A sigh slips out of him as he peels himself off me, clearly unhappy to put any distance between us.

"What has you so frustrated?" I ask, his eyes meeting mine. I could get lost in the warmth of them forever. Just another reason why I know marrying Leonard was the best thing I've ever done.

Apart from chasing my dream career, of course.

"I was debating how you are so very beautiful, but I haven't been able to come up with an answer," he says, making my heart flutter like a bird flapping its wings.

"Flattery won't get you out of answering my question," I remind him, even though every cell in my body is still dancing from his words.

"What if I don't want to tell you?" he asks, a hint of amusement playing in his eyes.

"You don't have to, but you want to," I say, making him nod several times because we both know I'm right.

"I just lost another potential investor," he explains. "The biggest one I had. Bolt Motors," Leonard adds, caressing my thighs with his thumbs.

"Fuck," I mumble, shock washing through me.

"Without them, I can't open the academy. Without them, I'm practically back to square one," he says, but I already knew that. Bolt Motors was the only big company that didn't call Leonard "out of his mind" for what he's trying to achieve.

They thought it was remarkable.

And they should, because it is.

"I'm so sorry, *amore*. I know how much you need them." Leonard rubs his nose along the column of my throat as I talk, and I try to ignore the tingles spreading through me where his lips brush my skin.

"It's okay. There will be others. I just have to find them, and I don't think I can do it alone," he says, not meaning alone as in without me, but alone in the sense of not having a business partner. While I'd love to be his partner, he needs someone else. He needs someone in racing who is like him. Who's walked a similar path of rejection and oppression.

"What about Valentina Romana? I thought you wanted to ask her," I say, his teeth grazing the sensitive skin just below my earlobe.

"She thinks I don't like her. How would I even start the conversation? 'Hey, Valentina. I know you think I hate you, but I actually don't. I'm just a grumpy arsehole, who is even grumpier when he's around you because it kills me that you haven't gotten a chance to race in F1, when you clearly more than deserve a seat, just because you're a woman and this sport is against women racing." He takes a deep breath once his rant is over, his frustration seeping off him with every quick, shallow breath.

"That's certainly one way to poach the subject," I suggest, but all it earns me is a frown from my husband.

"Ha ha, you are so bloody funny," he says before dropping his forehead against my sternum. "I have no idea what to do about any of this," he admits while I go back to playing with his hair. I love it when his hair is short and curly, and I know he likes it too because he keeps cutting it this way. I'm convinced it's because he likes it when I tug on the curls as he goes down on me.

"Well, *amore*, start with something small. How about opening yourself up to Valentina a bit more? I'm sure she could use a mentor and who better than you?" I ask, running my nails down his nape until he shivers, his fingers digging into my ass.

"If you want me to focus on this conversation, you're going to have to stop touching me like that," he warns, making me chuckle, which only rubs my chest even more against his face.

Leonard leans back in his seat to create some distance between us, his eyes trailing from my chest up to my face. A soft smile spreads over his mouth as he studies me, his bottom lip slipping between his teeth.

"What?" I ask.

"I'm thinking about how when this conversation is finished, I'm going to put you on your desk and bury my tongue inside of you." I shake my head, a blush settling on my cheeks without permission.

"You're unbelievable," I say, but I slide a little higher up on his lap to bring my needy pussy toward his growing bulge. I love feeling how much I turn him on without doing anything other than existing. "Focus," I remind him, and Leonard lets out a groan, slipping his hands onto my thighs and squeezing them.

"How do I open myself up?" he asks, his eyes glazed over with lust as they trail over the swell of my breasts, the way my nipples pebble against the thin fabric of my blouse.

"Befriend her. Offer her guidance. I know it's hard because you feel powerless, but maybe there will be a way you can help her get a spot at an academy in the future," I say, and he gives me a few nods. "Promise me you'll try. I don't like the way you let her think you hate her when you just want to help her," I add, so he lifts his pinky into the air, wiggling it until I wrap mine around his. Then, we touch our thumbs together, completing the circle to make sure this promise can't be broken.

"Everybody thinks I hate them. That's just my face," he replies, making me burst into laughter.

"You do have that 'go fuck yourself' look plastered on your features 24/7," I tease, causing him to tickle my sides until I squeal, wiggling on top of him to avoid his vengeance-seeking fingers.

"Actually, when I look at you, I have my 'come fuck me' face on, hoping you'll do exactly that." Leonard smirks at me. That damn smirk that has my entire body vibrating with need.

"I'm at work, husband. I can't do what you want me to do," I remind him, but Leonard merely lifts me off his lap and onto the desk behind me. He spreads my legs before placing one on each of his shoulders. A giggle escapes me, which causes his smirk to deepen.

"Then I'll fuck you instead. Would that be better, wife?" He licks his lips, forcing another giggle from me.

"Yes, I think that'd be just fine," I reply, swiping everything off my desk so I can lean back. Leonard's mouth immediately moves to my drenched panties, his nose running over where my clit is begging for attention.

"You smell like…" He trails off as he presses a kiss to my covered pussy.

"Your favorite meal. Yes, I know." He chuckles as he pushes my panties out of the way. "Well, go ahead. Make me come. If you can," I tease, forever taunting my man because it's hard to get rid of a habit that pushed us together our entire lives.

"Oh, I'll make you come, Chiara Tick. First on my mouth, then on my cock. But I need you to stay quiet for me. Your moans are mine and mine alone," he says, his possessive side slipping through as he runs a single finger over my pussy.

"Yes, sir," is my only reply before slamming my hand over my mouth to keep everyone at the gallery from finding out that my husband has his mouth on me while they're admiring the art I worked so hard on.

CHAPTER 12
Leonard

It's the first race weekend of the season, and Quinn and I are officially bickering over whether or not I have to attend yet another of those dreadful media conferences. I hate them. I hate being around most of the reporters. I hate answering the same questions over and over. I hate never being asked anything of value.

I'm always the one that gets the ridiculous questions.

"Hey, cheer up, mate. I'm here now," Adrian Romana says as he approaches Quinn and me. "There's no time to frown when you're in the presence of the greatest guy around," he adds with a cocky smile that makes his eyes sparkle with mischief.

"Arrogant arse," I mumble to Quinn, but she grins at Adrian with hearts in her eyes. She loves him. Everybody loves him. Hell, even I adore the kid more than I'll ever admit. It doesn't change how full of himself he is, though.

"There's no time for flattery, Leonard. We have to go and be interviewed," he says, winking at me before disappearing inside with a skip in his step. James Landon walks up to us, following behind Adrian.

"I can't keep up with him today. He's all over the place," he says, shaking his head. "If I didn't know better, I'd think he drank a bucket of coffee," James teases with a soft smile before walking after his best friend. "Wait up, you wanker." I almost snort at James' words.

"Oh, careful, Leonard. Your stone façade is breaking." Quinn nudges my shoulder with an amused eyebrow cocked so high, it almost touches her hairline.

"It'll never break for anyone but Chiara," I assure her, but it only makes her laugh.

"You keep telling yourself that, kiddo, but Adrian has started chipping away at that ice block around your heart long ago, and you know it," she says, shrugging like nothing of what she just said is terrifying at all.

"That bloody Adrian," I curse, grunting in complaint before walking into the conference room as well.

Gabriel Biancheri, who's going into his third year of racing in F1, sits on one of the couches, waiting patiently for the rest of us to join him. Cameron Kion, his best friend from what I've gathered over the years, is already beside him as they talk about something that has the Australian's jaw dropping to the floor.

An arm flings around my shoulders before I even make it another step into the room.

"Back again, are we?" I ask Adrian, who gives me a wicked smile.

"I need to tell you something," he says, not answering my question.

"I'm not sure I want to hear it," I reply, but Adrian merely loosens his grip on me a little as we step toward the couches.

"I got a very exciting message this morning."

That piques my curiosity, but the little shit doesn't explain himself at first. He leaves it at that, attempting to keep me in the dark by walking away, but I grab him by the elbow. The urge to smack him upside the back of his head is quite appealing, but I somehow manage to hold back.

"Tell me, or I'll kick the information out of you," I warn, forcing a chuckle out of him. I don't return it.

"I love it when you flirt with me," he says, so I finally smack him, but only his chest. He doesn't even flinch. Probably because of all those muscles he works so hard on every day just so he can keep looking like… well, like him.

"Be serious. What was the message?" I ask, hearing how curious I sound but unable to dial it down. He looks excited, and I want to be excited for my friend.

"Grenzenlos and Velocità Rossa are interested in signing me for next season." For the first time in my life in Formula One, my jaw fucking drops.

"They want you? Are they alright?" I tease, and, of course, the sunshine boy in front of me bursts into laughter.

"That's what I asked!" He wipes away his tears of laughter before puffing out his chest a little, pride making him smirk at me. "They must have finally seen how amazing I am. Smart people." He winks, and I wonder how anyone is able to breathe when they're in the same room as him and his massive ego.

"GET DOWN!" someone screams right as a massive bird flies inside. I barely duck in time to keep it from smashing into my head.

"What the hell?" I mumble, my eyes catching the black-feathered creature as it almost slams into Cameron Kion. The Australian throws himself off the couch and onto the floor to avoid the bird, Gabriel Biancheri laughing the entire time. Right until the bird moves from the back of the couch to his head. Then, it's Cameron's turn to laugh.

"Can someone help me?" the Monegasque asks, his body paralysed by fear. "Somebody please get this fucking bird off my head," he adds when no one moves a single millimetre. Adrian is flat on his arse laughing, James takes a step away, and the reporters that are already here don't move either.

"For fuck's sake," I say, rushing toward the kid and shooing the bird off his head.

I'm fucking terrified of birds, but I know what it feels like to have one sitting on you, thanks to Chiara and that little starling bird that follows her around all of

London. She's convinced it's her father looking out for her, and it's hard to argue considering it follows her *everywhere*.

"You alright?" I ask right as Gabriel deflates in his seat. The bird, a raven, lands on one of the big cameras a reporter from *Griffin Sports* brought in, looking around like it isn't scaring every single person in the room.

"Yeah, thanks," Gabriel says. His hair is all over the place and his hands are trembling, but Cameron is still laughing, utterly oblivious to his best friend's shock.

"Cameron, get it together," I bark, turning to see Adrian approaching me.

"We should get out of here, let the officials deal with this," he says, grabbing Gabriel's arm and helping him up.

"Media session is suspended. Drivers, you can go back to your teams' motorhomes. Reporters, I apologise, but there won't be a Q and A session today," the representative of the FIA says, signalling for everyone to get out.

"Oh no, media day is canceled. How horrible," Adrian says, sarcasm dripping from his words.

He hates media days. He thinks they're a waste of his precious time. Okay, maybe he also hates them now after I've told him how often reporters have twisted my words to make me look like an arse. Sometimes, people decide to debunk those articles with clips of the conference, but other times, people use this opportunity to shit on me as much as possible. They even throw in things from years ago that they haven't had a chance to bring up in a while.

The more I think about it, the clearer it gets that Adrian only started hating the media days after I told him this story. He loves the spotlight too much to hate it for any other reason. And the more I realise how good of a friend he is, the harder it gets for me to keep breathing, because no one in this sport has ever cared so much about me.

I don't think I'll ever get used to it.

"Are you thinking about me, old man? 'Cause you got that dreamy look in your eyes which is usually reserved for me," he says, ruining the moment I was having with him, albeit in my head.

"No, he was definitely thinking about me," Cameron Kion chimes in, and I barely restrain myself from calling the lot of them something not very nice and leaving again.

"Actually, I was thinking of the day I retire and don't have to see any of you again." I'm joking entirely, which is another problem in and of itself.

"I hate to break it to you, but you're stuck with me forever, Leonard. There is no escaping. You can run, but you can't hide from our friendship. From *me*." Adrian's words are followed by an evil laugh like a villain laughs after telling the hero their plan to destroy the world. I almost shudder. Then, I almost burst into laughter.

"You, kiddo, need to relax," I suggest, but the Monegasque merely shrugs.

"Perhaps." He leaves without another word.

My eyes shift to James and Gabriel, who glare at each other for a moment before heading in two separate directions. The tension between them gets worse every single time I see them. Old me wouldn't have given a single fuck about what's happening between the two of them. New me, the version Chiara and Adrian turned me into, really wants to know what happened to make them hate each other so much.

Or *who* happened.

Quinn and I have been standing next to my new Grenzenlos F1 car for the last twenty minutes, discussing our Quali strategy with my race engineer. The car has been feeling amazing for the past two days. I was fastest in the first and third free practice, but Jonathan has gotten his act back under control and finished in second, first, and second place.

In other words, Grenzenlos has the potential to dominate for another season, but Jonathan might be a problem for my chance to get my third and last championship title.

"We'll go with the soft tyres last. First, let's try the medium," Riley says, and I give them a curt nod. I'm only half listening. The other half of my brain drifts to my wife.

My wife, who didn't come to the first race because she has an appointment with her gynecologist to see if everything's alright or if there's a reason we've been trying to get pregnant but it hasn't happened yet. My wife, who has to go through that alone because I'm not there. My wife, who I love more than life itself.

Her appointment was supposed to start ten minutes ago, so all my brain *wants* to think about is her. All I'm *allowed* to think about is racing.

"We only have two sets of softs left for this weekend, so we have to be careful not to overuse them during Quali, okay?" Riley adds, their voice firm. It's a warning, but I'm not planning on ruining an entire set of tyres to get pole.

"Alright," is my only response. I'm hoping it'll get them to move on to their next responsibility so I can check my phone and see if there is an update from Chiara.

Once Riley leaves, I turn to my best friend, but she shakes her head before I can even phrase my question.

"Nothing yet, sorry," Quinn says as if she read my mind.

I don't get a chance to wait for an update. Quinn hands me my balaclava and helmet, then my gloves. She ushers me into the car, and I do as I'm told. The faster this session is over, the faster I can call Chiara.

Qualifying is a fucking mess.

Halfway through the session, rain starts pouring down, the drops so big, a single one could be a sip of water. I'm drenched by the time Q3 comes around. Quinn looks concerned, but I think Riley keeps assuring her it'll be fine because they place a comforting hand on her shoulder every time my best friend shakes her head and says something.

Q3 gets postponed for ten minutes, all of us waiting for the rain to slow enough so visibility increases. In the meantime, I ask Quinn to check on Chiara, but there's no update yet. The worry in my chest multiplies by a million, my body itching to get out of the car and fly back home.

My priorities have shifted immensely since Chiara and I became everything. In other words, she became my priority. Chiara, Benz, and our perfect little life.

The rain slows fifteen minutes later, and Q3 starts. My chest is heavy with concern the entire time I'm on the track, but the feeling gets pushed away a little when Riley tells me Jonathan is on provisional pole.

Fuck.

That.

I take a deep breath during my last out lap, getting ready to grab the first pole of the season. Jonathan won't take it from me. Chiara is at home, counting on me to succeed even when she isn't here. And although she jump-started my love for racing by *coming* to the races, she's still fuelling my passion from far away.

So, I'll get the first pole of the season.

I'll make my wife proud.

With rain still hitting my visor and the wet tyres barely able to keep me from sliding, I speed down the straight, over the start line. Racing in the wet is tricky, and, unlike Adrian, I don't excel at it. It takes more out of me, more concentration and caution.

"Lots of water build-up in corner ten. Careful or you'll slip," Riley warns, but I already knew that. I felt it during my warm-up lap.

"First sector?" I ask when I enter the second one, groaning as I fight with my car to stay on track in the proper racing line.

"Purple."

Purple is good.

Purple means I'm improving.

Purple says I have a chance to get pole.

"Second sector?" I barely manage to breathe out the words.

"Green."

Usually, I wouldn't ask and Riley doesn't tell me until my lap is done—unless I'm very far behind and finishing the lap is useless—but I have to know.

"Push, Leonard!" Riley barks, and I let out one more groan as I twist my steering wheel to take the last corner. The G-force threatens to crush me, but I don't crumble under the pressure. I use every last muscle I have and race down the straight over the finish line again. "You did it! Pole position, man!"

"*Woohooo*, come on!" I scream, joy filling me from top to bottom.

"Adrian got third place," Riley informs me during my cool-down lap because they know it will only intensify my happy feelings.

My pride.

Adrian has won the occasional race over the last few years, but his car at Spark has never been quick enough in Quali to be in the top three.

Until today.

Adrian practically jumps out of his car as soon as the drivers that got the top three positions have parked their cars in their designated spots. He skips my way, flinging his arms around me in a hug. I return it with a lot less hesitancy than I would have years ago. He releases me quickly, running toward where his sister, Valentina, is standing with the rest of his team. She smiles brightly at her brother, and he hugs her to his chest over the barrier. Helmet still on, he nudges her temple with his head before moving on to the rest of his team.

I walk toward Quinn and my team, and she shows me my phone as subtly as she can so I can see the message Chiara sent.

Chiara: The doctor said everything looks fine. It sometimes just takes a while, which means as soon as you get home, we should keep trying. Over and over.

I burst into laughter of relief and pure joy, glad no one can see my face or record it before hugging Quinn and celebrating this amazing day with the rest of my crew.

CHAPTER 13
Leonard

My engine caught fire.

The high I was on yesterday after qualifying, the one I did my best to carry over into today, vanishes into thin smoke as I jump out of my F1 car and run away from it. I spin around to see the marshals extinguish the flames, smoke filling the air all around us. My heart sinks at the sight, and I lose all feeling in my legs. I sink into a squat, the breath rushing out of me until I'm almost hyperventilating.

For one, your car catching fire with you in it is fucking terrifying.

Two, starting the season with a burning engine ending your race is far from ideal.

Actually, it's the fucking worst because not only does it feel like I failed as a driver, but my team is going to be horribly disappointed.

The media will tear Grenzenlos and me apart until we feel even more like shit. Robert Fuchs is going to throw his headphones to a different dimension in anger, which will be turned into another joke by the reporters and fans.

I mean, afterward, it's pretty funny, but we have to get there first.

For now, I haven't managed to get up from my squatting position. I haven't regained the feeling in my legs. I haven't found a way to stop staring at where my car is up in flames.

This is supposed to be the season I get my third championship. This is supposed to be it. But all it is right now is a mess.

A hot, burning mess.

Literally.

"Mr. Tick, are you alright?" a marshal asks. I look up right as her hand wraps around my arm, attempting to help me up.

"I need another moment." To catch my breath. To keep from hyperventilating. To process what the fuck just happened.

The first race of the season has gone to shit.

What the fuck am I going to do if the rest of it goes the same way?

"Fuck me, this is so nice," Adrian says as he stretches his long legs out in front of him in my private jet. "I've never been on a private plane before, but I could definitely get used to this," he adds, smirking at one of the stewardesses as she walks by. She blushes immediately, looking over her shoulder at the heartbreaker. "Definitely," Adrian repeats, mumbling more to himself than he is speaking to me.

"Do you ever turn off that... that part of yourself?" I ask, pointing at all of him. He cocks a curious brow at me.

"Are you jealous?" he teases, his smirk now directed my way.

"Of what?"

"My attention drifting to someone else. You can have it all, mate, but you're gonna have to entertain me for the next ten hours if you want my undivided attention." He crosses his arms in front of his chest, his eyes staring directly into mine. He looks so smug, so full of himself, I wonder for the millionth time how anyone could be this confident.

"Nah, go for it. But I should warn you, the bathroom is not the most comfortable of places to fuck," I say, catching too late exactly what I'm sharing with the nosy man in front of me.

Adrian practically beams at me, his sunshine smile on full blast.

"And how the hell do you know *that*?" he asks, the toe of his shoe poking my shin. I stay silent, so he kicks me again. "I have ten hours and you have limited space to avoid me, so you might as well fess up." I lean back in my seat, crossing my legs over one another as I watch him for a moment.

"Everywhere in here. Especially where you're sitting." All amusement leaves him.

"Please tell me you had it cleaned."

I shake my head without hesitation, even if it's a lie. The colour drains from his face as he undoes his seatbelt to stand up.

"That's very unhygienic, Leonard. What the fuck?" I burst into laughter at his disgusted face, and the sound surprises him so much, he freezes in place to just stare at me. "Did you just—" He cuts off, disbelief painting his features. "I need to sit back down, but I don't know where," he says, which only makes me laugh even harder.

I don't know what has come over me, but I can't stop.

"Stop, you're scaring me," he says, settling back down in the seat across from mine.

"The whole jet got a deep clean, kiddo, relax," I say right as Valentina, Adrian's sister, steps out of the washroom.

"This bathroom is huge! It's bigger than the one I have at Aunt Carolina's house," she says, smiling to herself before directing her happy look at her brother. He returns it because of course he does. They're both such sunshines, even after all the pain they've experienced. All the pain they still go through every single day.

"Leonard and I were just talking about the bathroom actually." It's my turn to kick him under the table then. "Ow. Dickhead," he says, rubbing his leg and glaring at me.

Valentina doesn't seem to notice, merely grabs her book and plops down in her seat, the one on the other side of the aisle. She shoves her earphones into her ears and taps her fingers against the side of her book.

I stare at her young face for a moment, all her hopes and dreams reflected in her eyes. Along with rejections. The sadness of having been turned away from the sport she loves so much all her life. She's just a kid, yet she's known so many struggles. So much devastation and grief, and not even her dream can be her lifeline when she keeps getting told she isn't good enough.

"I know," Adrian says, sadness now lingering in his eyes as he looks at his sister, too. She's immersed in her book, her legs pulled to her chest on the seat, drowning in an oversized hoodie. "She deserves better. She deserves everything, and I don't know how to give her the world when the world keeps slipping through my fingertips right as I'm about to hand it to her."

Adrian stops talking to stare down at his hands, his shoulders dropping in defeat.

"She fights so hard to get the same chances every guy would have gotten long ago with her talent, dedication, and skill. The only thing in her way are stupid societal norms and expectations." His eyes lift to my face, studying me. "What can I do to help her? You must have some kind of idea," he says, almost begging now.

"There's nothing you can do that you haven't done before, Adrian. But I'm going to help you. And her. I'm looking for ways, for driver academies, that have a good heart and as much faith in Valentina as we do. They just need a little push, and I'll shove them down the fucking cliff if I have to."

This makes my sunshine friend smile again, and thank God because seeing Adrian sad is one of the worst things for me. It's unsettling.

"I didn't know you even liked my sister, let alone would commit a crime for her."

"She's your sister, which makes her family." Feeling like I've said too much already, I shut my mouth, pulling at a loose thread in my shirt.

"Then why do you act like you don't like her?" Adrian challenges, knowing that there's something I'm hiding.

Fortunately for him, I do like sharing my feelings with him.

"I can't look at her without feeling my chest constrict. There's nothing I can do to help, and I hate how powerless it makes me feel. With others, I can make a plan and find a solution to their problems. With Valentina, I see myself in her, and that powerless feeling? The one I felt throughout my entire childhood and teenage years? I hate that feeling. So, I don't look at her. I barely speak to her. I'm looking for a way, a solution, but until I have one, spending time with her just brings up old things I haven't dealt with yet."

My rant comes to an end, Adrian's jaw is so far on the floor, I can see all of his teeth. I lean forward and push his chin up, closing his mouth again.

"There's more to me than my outer, grumpy layer, kiddo." He shakes his head in disbelief.

"I know there is, but I still get mesmerized every time you share how you feel with me. I hope you know I don't take that for granted. Quite the opposite. I'm honored."

It'll never cease to amaze me how genuine this man is. He cares *so much*. More than anyone I've ever met, except for Chiara.

I get why he's never let anyone in romantically.

The way he gives himself over to someone fully, wholeheartedly... it would destroy him if they left.

So, he doesn't let anyone close to his heart.

I just hope he's reserving it for the right one instead of locking it behind bars for life.

"Promise me that one day, when the right person steps into your life, you stop running from the possibility of love," I say, catching him completely off-guard.

"What the fuck are you talking about?" he asks with a laugh, but I can see in his eyes how raw of a wound my words have dug their claws into.

"Don't laugh it off. I mean it. I know you're scared. I know falling in love after getting hurt over and over in your life is the last thing you want, but *you*—you personally, not everyone in this world—need to find someone you can love. Otherwise, all that potential, that huge heart inside of you, it goes to waste. It goes to waste or, worse, it will destroy you for not allowing it to love as freely as it would like to."

Tears shoot into his eyes, and he tries to blink them away, but he isn't fast enough.

"A head and a heart don't always agree. Hell, most of the time, they don't. But you cannot let your head keep you from experiencing this part of life forever. You're human. You're made to feel everything life has to offer. Don't just let your heart feel the bad, the pain, the grief. Let it feel love, Adrian."

A single tear drops down his cheek, but he wipes it away and blows out a breath.

"You and your words can go fuck yourself, Leonard." He bursts into laughter when I give him an unimpressed look.

"Promise me," I say, but he shakes his head.

"I can't." His voice is barely more than a whisper.

"Would you want her to close her heart off?" I ask, pointing at Valentina, who's giggling at something in her book.

"She'd be safer that way. Do you know how many times I caught her crying over her feelings for Gabriel when she thought I didn't see? Do you know how longingly she looks after him? He will break her heart one way or another, and she will be devastated. If I could protect her from that, don't you think I'd do everything I could?" he says, leaning forward to make sure Valentina doesn't hear him under any circumstance, even with her music playing in her ears.

"You'd keep her from living her life? From finding her soulmate? From potentially meeting someone and growing her family? From sharing all that love she holds in her heart?" He sinks into his seat, silence filling the space between us.

"No," he eventually replies, conceding.

"Then don't be a little shit and do that to yourself," I say, earning another frown from him.

"Fine, you stubborn asshole." Content, I almost smile at him, which only irritates him more. "Do you always get off on being right?"

"No, but I'm married to Chiara, who is always right about everything. It's nice when I get to be right and smug," I explain, wiggling my brows at him. He flips me off before getting up and walking toward Valentina, hugging her head to his chest.

My eyes drift from them to the book in her hand, reminding me I have to finish the last few chapters of Chiara's and my buddy read.

I dig around in my backpack for it, my eyes skimming the title as I place it on the table in front of me.

I picked a romantasy this time, one she's been meaning to read for almost a year, and I love the way she keeps giggling at everything the male main character says to the female main character.

Fuck, I love my life.

I love my wife even more.

CHAPTER 14

Chiara

Five more races have passed since the first race where Leonard DNFed because of an engine problem. My husband won three of six races this season. Jonathan Kent, the man I've fantasized about cutting up into little pieces and feeding them to Benz, won the others. Grenzenlos has been dominating once again, but Jonathan is currently leading the championship, which has been pissing Leonard off, and rightfully so.

I'm also pissed.

That slimy, rude, full-of-himself *figlio di puttana* can choke on his disgusting personality.

If it were up to me, I'd have shoved it down his throat years ago, but Leonard told me we had to play nice for the media. The media which hates Leonard. The media which has turned so many people against him I've received death threats just for existing. It's why I haven't gone to any race since the second one this season.

People were messaging me on social media, threatening to find me and...

I shudder at the reminder.

While I can defend myself and most of those people are all bark, no bite, Leonard and I have agreed that until it comes down to it, the last race or the one to decide the championship for good, I'd stay at home, where I'm safe. Out of the spotlight.

It fascinates me how people will just *ruin* things. For no reason. I love watching Leonard race. I love being at his races to support him, but there is no way in hell I'd make him worry about me when he should be focusing on his performance during his last season at Grenzenlos.

So, they won.

Everyone who wanted to scare me away from the race weekends won.

I hope they're proud of themselves.

"You wear my ring. Your name is tattooed across my left pec. And yet, every single time I look at you, I can't believe you're really mine," Leonard says right as I hang the last star from the ceiling in my second exhibition room. For a while, I'd taken down my starry immersive piece, but upon popular request, I've decided to bring it back.

"Tattooing my name on your chest was a bad idea. I told you that," I reply with a smile, stepping down from the ladder. He wraps his arms around me and pulls me off before I can place my foot on the second to last step, a giggle escaping me as I pull my legs up to avoid accidentally kicking his shins.

"It was the best idea. Your name belongs there, right on my chest above the heart that is entirely yours." My husband places me back on my feet only to spin me around and capture my lips with his. "And there's still space for some other names, too." He breaks the kiss only long enough to speak, then goes straight back to placing his lips on mine.

His hands drop to my ass, which is barely covered in the shorts I decided to wear today to make my exhibits. I moan into his mouth without meaning to because I can't help myself. I love the way it feels when his tongue slips between my teeth and into my mouth. I love how his hard body rubs against mine. I love the way he kisses me like I'm truly the sweetest poison he's ever tasted, corrupting him in the best way possible.

"I have to finish this room. People are expecting to see the new-old immersive piece when they come tomorrow." His lips drop to my neck, his teeth grazing my sensitive skin there.

"I want to make *you* come *now*."

My heart skips several beats from his words and the way he runs his tongue over my neck, tasting me. My entire body catches fire, an ache appearing between my legs.

"Let me make you come, and then I'll help you finish this room," he offers, his hands dropping to the back of my thighs to lift me into the air and wrap my legs around his waist.

"Leonard," I gasp, my hands sliding onto his nape to hold onto him.

"Please, baby. Please let me."

"God, I love it when you beg," I say. "Put your mouth on—" We're interrupted by the sound of a voice coming from the main room.

A voice I haven't heard in years.

"Chiara de Luca?" he says, and Leonard's back stiffens.

"Why can no one ever get your name right?" he grumbles, and I almost laugh as I wiggle out of his grip so my feet can drop back on the ground.

"Maybe because we didn't tell the entire world we got married?" I remind him, making him groan more. "Wait here, I'll deal with Dino," I add, kissing his cheek and attempting to walk away when his fingers snake around my forearm, holding me back.

"Dino? The wanker who didn't want to invest in your dream? I'll fucking deal with him, little demon." Leonard storms out of the room and, slightly turned on, I watch his ass as he walks away, enjoying how riled up he gets when it comes to protecting me.

"Mr. Tick, it's a pleasure to—" Leonard cuts him off right as I step into the main room.

"I'm going to give you five seconds to leave. If you're not gone by then, I swear I'll take that sign behind me that says 'Meteorite' and I'll hit you over the head with it for what you did to my wife." Dino's eyes go wide at the threat, so I press my lips together to keep from laughing. I don't want to laugh in Dino's presence.

He wasn't responsible for what happened at the exhibit I planned at one of his galleries, the one I worked on for months—that was all on Tim—but he didn't even give me a second chance. He judged my art based on the scandal he didn't prevent by ensuring no one would mess with my laptop. After dangling a dream opportunity in front of me, he snatched it away without hesitation. Without blinking an eye. When we first met, I thought he was nice. I liked him, albeit not in a romantic way since, well, Leonard has always preoccupied my heart too much for anyone else to take it.

"Wife? Oh, I didn't know you two got married. Congratulations," Dino says, ignoring Leonard's scowl and the threat upon his life.

"We did, but we'd appreciate it if you didn't tell anyone," I say, stepping beside Leonard to take his hand in mine. He relaxes slightly, but he never looks away from Dino. "If you're here to cry over the missed opportunity of not investing in me before I was making a fuckton of money, save it. I don't need your help anymore." His eyes sparkle with amusement at my words, and he even smiles at me, though it's a little wobbly because Leonard's gaze has turned darker with rage.

"Actually, I am here to propose a new business arrangement. To expand your brand across Europe. I have some art galleries that are now vacant because the previous artist who was exhibiting their work has sadly given up art. So, I have three places that desperately need an artist to fill them with their creativity."

I take a step back without meaning to, and Leonard immediately moves in front of me, protecting me from whatever I need distance from. His arm snakes around me from the front, his hand slipping onto my hip.

"That's a huge opportunity," I say, looking at Dino. His gaze is stuck on Leonard, eyeing him like my husband is about to tackle him to the ground and beat him up.

"It is, and seeing what you've made of this place, I'm convinced you'd thrive," he replies, pointing around the room.

"How much of the profits would go to Chiara?" Leonard asks, ever the business-man.

"Fifty-fifty?" Dino asks with a smile. I cock a challenging brow.

"How about ninety-ten?" I cross my arms in front of my chest. "I'd be the one putting all the work in, after all."

"But I'm providing the space, so let's say seventy-five percent for you, twenty-five for me. How does that sound?"

"Sounds like something I should discuss with my husband, but thank you for the offer. We'll be in touch once I've made my decision," I reply, and he gives me another easy smile.

"I expected nothing less. I'll have the official offer to you in a day so you can know all of the details as you make your decision," Dino says and steps back. "And thank you for not following through on your threat," he adds as he looks at Leonard.

"Well, not yet, but make no mistake, you do anything to upset Chiara, and I'll destroy you. Without hesitation." Leonard's fingers squeeze my hip possessively, and I almost melt into his touch.

"You got it."

Dino offers me a goodbye in Italian, then turns around to leave my art gallery.

Once the door is closed, I step toward it, locking it before leaning against it to look at Leonard.

"We need to talk about this offer," he says, and I nod in agreement.

"After," I reply.

He's still frowning, but when I reach for my oversized shirt and pull it over my head, his gaze softens and a smirk tugs at the corner of his mouth. I rip my sports bra off next and shimmy out of my shorts until I'm only in my panties.

"You want me on my knees, sweetheart?" he asks, but I shake my head.

"No. I want you to be in control. Do whatever you want, as long as you're rough." I take my hair out of its bun, letting it drop to the top of my shoulders.

"You do know there are cameras in here?" he asks as he removes his shirt, his chest now on full display for me.

"Perfect. We can watch the recording later."

He has me off my feet and pinned against the wall a second later.

CHAPTER 15

Leonard

It's the last race before the summer break, and I've extended my lead in the championship to thirty points. I'm excited to finally have a break from being away from Chiara. It's been almost two weeks since I last saw her in person because she decided to take Dino up on his offer, so she's been in Milan to get started on filling the gallery with her ideas and pieces of art.

To say it's been slowly killing me being away from her might be dramatic... but it's also very much how I've been feeling. I hate being away from Chiara for so long, especially while she's thriving and happy. I want to be right by her side when she feels this way to soak in all of the positive feelings. Seeing her happy makes my entire being feel like it's floating among the fucking clouds, high and light as a feather.

Today, I feel as heavy as a bag of bricks.

"Cheer up, mate! You are in fantastic company," Adrian says as we make our way toward where the national anthem of Monaco will be sung. "I know you're pissed I got pole yesterday, but it's my home country, so it means more to me and you should be happy for me." He's grinning hard now.

Since he got pole yesterday, he hasn't stopped smiling. Spark Racing is our closest rival this season with Velocità Rossa right behind them, too. He has a chance to win today, and as much as it pains me that I'm going to fight him for the win—a win which would mean more to him since this is his home race—it's not in a Formula One driver's nature to give up a first place. Even if it's for a friend.

"I *am* happy for you. Doesn't mean I'll take it easy on you," I reply, nudging his shoulder with mine.

"Ha! Overtaking is extremely difficult on this track and, unless my team fucks up our strategy or I make a mistake, which never happens, this win is mine. Try and stop me," he challenges, puffing out his chest a little. His smile never fades, doesn't even drop a little.

"Don't worry, we're all going to," James chimes in, wrapping an arm around Adrian's shoulders. "No one wants to be in the same room with someone who announces they're going to win and then really win. You're cocky enough as is." I snort at the accuracy of James' comment.

"It's a bloody wonder he hasn't suffocated us all already," I mumble, earning a laugh from James.

"Alright, I don't know why I've become both of your punching bags, but not even you two can bring me down on a day like today. Prepare to be sick of me because *when* I win, I'll never shut up about it," Adrian says, skipping ahead to where Cameron is standing. In one swift jump, the Monegasque throws himself against the Australian's back. I hear an *oomph* from Cameron before Adrian places his legs around him in a piggyback position.

"Mate, you are almost twice my height. We're gonna fall if you don't get off," Cameron warns, but all I hear in response is Adrian's deep laughter.

"Hey, do you mind if I ask you a racing question?" I turn to James, my brows furrowing in confusion.

"*You* want to ask *me* a racing question?" I can't hide my surprise, no matter how much I try. None of the other drivers—apart from the chaotic man still on Cameron's back—have ever asked me for advice in this sport. They usually stay clear of me like I'm a bad case of the flu they don't want to catch.

"Yeah, if that's alright with you." I stop walking, studying his genuine expression before shaking my head to force my mind to focus on what he wants to talk about. If I'm good at anything, it's helping people, even ones I never expected would ask me for any help.

"Yeah, of course. What's your question?"

James and I end up talking for several minutes about his question on late-breaking combined with overtaking on this track. Most of the conversation is me saying "Don't fucking do it, but if you have to, here is how" while he nods along to my words. If I didn't know better, I'd say he's hanging onto every single one of them, making sure he doesn't miss anything that comes out of my mouth.

"Does that make sense?" I ask when I'm finally done explaining.

"Yeah, thank you," he replies, his hands trembling a little as he zips up his racing suit all the way.

"Is everything okay with you, James? You seem nervous." I don't know why I care, but seeing a driver's hands shaking before the start of a race is never a good sign. He needs to be focused, in control of his feelings, and I won't have it on my conscience if something happens and I didn't ask him if he's alright.

And because he's Adrian's best friend, but I'd never admit that to anyone.

"I'm not the biggest fan of street circuits, not since my big crash here a few years ago," he explains, avoiding eye contact.

He digs his heels into the ground as if he could move the cement as if it were sand. For a moment, silence engulfs us as we step toward the other drivers. I place a hand on his arm before we get into Adrian and Cameron's earshot.

"I understand that fear, the one that lingers after an accident like yours. But fear is far more dangerous in our sport. Any type of uncertainty or lack of confidence in yourself and your race can end badly for you. You have to let it go. You can't let it control you. You're a great racer. Trust yourself to have learned from your mistakes."

James lets out a deep breath, his blue eyes filling with determination.

"Good, that's better." I almost offer him a reassuring smile when I think better of it.

"Thank you, Leonard. Means a lot," James replies, a shy blush settling on his cheeks. "You were my hero when I was growing up, you know? I always wanted to be like you. Great. Invincible. A legend."

"You're still young, James, you'll get there," I assure him, placing a hand on his shoulder and squeezing it.

"You think so?" he asks, still blushing.

A shiver of unease runs through me. I've never been a driver's hero before.

Adrian doesn't see me as a hero. He sees me as a friend, confidant, and mentor perhaps. Not a hero, not the driver he looked up to since he was a kid. I have no idea what to do with this level of admiration.

I don't know if I'm worthy of it, but I'm going to do my best to be.

"Yeah, I do. Just stay focused. You will get your seat at one of the big teams sooner or later." The smile following my words is so bright, I consider pulling out my sunglasses to shield my eyes from it.

"Thanks, mate."

Adrian grabs his best friend's attention by dropping off Cameron's back and announcing, "Oh, shoot, looks like Gabriel and I have been given a separate area to stand on," he starts and winks at us. "Monaco really knows how to celebrate their F1 drivers." He skips away without another word, and I exchange a look with James.

Unfortunately for us, he is right. Gabriel and Adrian are standing in front of all the other drivers where the organizers of the Grand Prix placed large posters of their faces on the ground. No wonder Adrian is the way he is. His home country, hell, the whole world, worships him. Of course, he's full of himself.

How could he not be?

If I'd get even a fraction of the love he receives daily, I'd have a God complex.

And, suddenly, Adrian Romana makes complete sense to me.

We're halfway through the race.

Adrian is still leading, and Gabriel Biancheri has made his way into third place, fighting off my teammate. The Monegasque's Zeitgeist has an advantage on this track that our Grenzenlos is missing. It's quick in the corners. We have a speed advantage in the straights, but since there are eighteen corners and this track is quite short, Gabriel has made up a lot of time. He started in fourth, but Jonathan, being as slow as he is, slept at the start and lost his place to the driver who's currently in the talks for a Velocità Rossa seat for next year.

Adrian is being considered to replace me or also go to Velocità Rossa, but they're still fighting over him. Robert Fuchs hardly told me anything about the negotiations, only that Kyle Hughes, a rookie currently driving for Klein Racing, is also on their radar for next season.

My gut tells me summer break is going to be filled with Formula One drama, and I can't wait to be as far away from it as possible for a few weeks.

"Leonard, we're going with strategy C," Riley informs me right after my pitstop.

Strategy C means to aim for second place because the Spark is too quick and we can't catch it. It means managing the tyres until the end of the race. I hate being told not to fight for first place, but I'd never do anything as stupid as risking my entire race for the win. Plus, Jonathan is struggling in fourth place, which means my championship lead will extend even more if I bring second place home.

"Gabriel is in the wall! Safety car deployed. Slow down." My heart skips several beats, shock rolling through my system.

"Is he okay?" I ask, breathing heavily from racing and worry.

"Yeah, he's okay. Muttered something like 'I am stupid' several times over the team radio," my race engineer says, so I nod to let that information process. The kid's fine. The race at his home Grand Prix has ended horribly, but at least he's okay. "Okay, red flag has been called for. Drive the car into the pits and then you can get out. His Zeitgeist is in a difficult position to extract, so it'll take a while."

And it does. It takes almost forty-five minutes to clear the car and debris. The restart goes well for Adrian, and he ends up winning the race, just as he predicted he would. I come in second with Jonathan in third, James in fourth, and Cameron in sixth.

As much as I was dreading Adrian's attitude after he brought this win home, I couldn't be happier for him. He jumps out of his car and bolts toward his team immediately, screaming in joy and bouncing all over the place. Happiness practically wafts off him, infecting me when he sprints my way to wrap his arms around me, too.

"I did it!" he announces, so I pat him on the back, telling him how well he drove. How much he deserves this win.

Monaco explodes into celebrations.

Even Gabriel comes out of the Zeitgeist garage to stand with Adrian's team and celebrate his fellow Monegasque's win. Something like this takes a lot of strength and a great personality, which is great to see in Formula One.

And, who knows, maybe those two will become teammates next season if Velocità Rossa manages to sign both of them.

I almost smile at the possibility.

Chapter 16

Chiara

Leonard has been in a horrible mood for the past week. Not with me. Never with me. But he's gotten another rejection from a possible sponsor for his driver academy, and he's getting quite discouraged about making his new dream happen.

Knowing my husband better than he even knows himself, I booked him an appointment at his favorite tattoo parlor. He's been wanting to get another hand tattoo for weeks, but he hasn't had the chance yet since he had to race. It takes a few weeks for it to heal enough for him to be able to put his gloves on or sweat, so the summer break is the perfect time for him to finally get it.

"Where are you taking me?" he asks as soon as we get into his newest Grenzenlos sports car.

"I'm going to cheer you up," is all I reply before putting the car into Drive and reversing out of the parking spot.

"You already did when you opened your eyes this morning, saw me, and smiled," he replies, making my heart flutter. "And then again when we took a shower together," Leonard adds, the smile on his lips perfectly smug. "Oh, are you finally taking me to a sex shop? I bet there are loads more things we could try out," he suggests. I can't help but grin.

"Maybe after. There's something else we're going to do first," I reply, shaking my head a little at his suggestion and the fact that I didn't think of it.

Leonard places his hand on my neck, rubbing his thumb along the sore area there. He loves massaging me every chance he gets. My back, arms, neck, legs, anywhere really. As if I'm the one constantly sore from training and racing, not him.

"Tell me where we're going, sweetheart. Help my curious mind settle," he begs, the sound oh so pretty.

"No." He groans in frustration but never stops rubbing my neck.

He drops the subject until I park the car, not even realizing where we are because he's too busy staring at me. His brown eyes, my favorite set of eyes, are full of love as he takes in every single centimeter of my face like he hasn't done so a thousand times already. I turn to him, cocking an eyebrow.

"Would you like to tell me why you're staring?" I ask, shutting off the engine by pressing the button beside the steering wheel.

"Your eyes are so green, they look like a malachite crystal. Your bottom lip is so full and plump, I want to bite it. Your smile is so breathtaking, all the oxygen in my lungs has vanished. That's why I'm staring, my wife." I blush under his gaze and from his words. "If I could, I'd connect our brains so you could always know just how deeply I love you. So you could know how much I worship you because I do, Chiara Tick. I worship the very ground you walk on," he says and leans forward to cup my cheeks in his hands. "Tell me you know that. Tell me I'm a good husband and make you feel everything I feel."

"You do," I whisper, closing the distance between our mouths to kiss him. "I wouldn't have married you if you didn't love me as fiercely as you do," I say against his lips, making him smile.

"You deserve nothing less." He captures my lips again, his tongue slipping into my mouth to taste me.

"Do you think how we feel will ever fade?" I ask, but Leonard merely smirks at me.

"I wouldn't see how, Starling. I vowed forever, and I meant it. You're mine and I'm yours until the end of time." He nudges my nose with his, making me giggle. "Now, tell me, where did you bring m—" He cuts off as he turns his head to see his favorite tattoo parlor right in front of us. "I've been more annoying about my hand tattoo than I thought if you're bringing me here just to shut me up." I burst into laughter.

"Yeah, you have been. Let's go, so I don't have to hear you talk about it anymore," I tease, but he chuckles, knowing full well that's not the reason we're here. He knows I want to make him as happy as he makes me. "So, what are you getting?" I ask as we step out of the car and walk toward the door. Leonard grabs my hand, lacing his fingers through mine.

"We'll decide together. It'll be your necklace, after all." I almost stumble over my own feet, my cheeks heating uncontrollably from his words.

Leonard opens the door for me, his hand slipping onto my lower back as he gently guides me inside and toward the front desk where Giustina, Leonard's tattoo artist, sits. She's also Italian, and, when I called the store a few days ago, we ended up speaking for a while about how different living in London is to living in Italy. She only moved here a few years ago, so she remembers far more than I do about living in our home country, and I had a great time listening to her stories.

"*Ciao*, Giustina, *come stai*?" I ask, moving away from Leonard's touch to extend a hand in greeting.

My husband grumbles at the loss of contact, but I ignore him, knowing that, in a moment, he'll find a way to put his hands back on me anyway. Either that, or I'll take one of his in mine.

Giustina's brown eyes light up at the sight of us, and she gets out of her chair to step in front of me.

"Chiara, it's so good to finally meet you," she replies in Italian, swatting my hand away to place kisses on my cheeks, the way Italians and many Europeans do. She turns to Leonard, still smiling. "She's even more beautiful than you described, and that's saying a lot." She throws me a look over her shoulder. "Blink twice if he blackmailed you into marriage," Giustina teases, her accent thick now that she's speaking English.

I blink twice just to spite my husband, but my evil smile tells a completely different story. Giustina bursts into laughter.

"Oh, I love her. Come, come, choose your design, or tell me what you had in mind and I'll draw it up for you," she offers, her attention on Leonard.

"My wife is going to choose today," he announces, and I almost choke on my breath.

"That's a terrible idea," I reply, but my husband only shrugs.

"I thought the same thing about kissing you, and now I can't stop. Terrible ideas can be a lot of fun," he says as he approaches me, wrapping his arms around me just to nuzzle his face into my neck and gently nibble on my sensitive skin. I giggle without meaning to, scowling at him when he steps back again.

"I didn't giggle," I say, pointing my finger at his chest. He raises his hands in mock surrender, but the smug look is back on his face. "I'm going to choose the ugliest tattoo for you," I mumble before following Giustina to where the binders with designs are.

None of the ones available have what I'm looking for, so I describe an idea for Giustina, who wastes no time drawing it up. I watch her e-pen fly over the screen of her iPad as she sketches and keeps asking me questions.

"What do you think?" she asks a few minutes later, turning the screen Leonard's and my way.

"It's perfect." I spin to look at Leonard. "Do you like it?" I ask, taking his right hand in mine.

"Can you print out the stencil and put it on? I want to see something," is his only response, his frown back in place.

"If you don't like it, we can try something else," I say, my excitement fading a little. He leans down to kiss my forehead.

"Let me just see it on my hand." I nod while he gives me another forehead kiss, making me feel all warm and tingly inside.

Giustina prints out the stencil before applying it to Leonard's hand. My husband can be very patient when he wants to be, and I almost laugh at the way he watches the stencil being placed on his hand. It's right on the curve between his index finger and thumb and snakes around both fingers. It's a chain like one of the necklaces Leonard has bought me in the past and right in the middle of the curve hangs a charm that spells "mine."

I roll my lips to fight a smile.

"I'm going to step out for a cigarette while you think about it. How does that sound?" Giustina asks, and Leonard gives an agreeing nod.

"Sounds great."

He waits for her to step out of the room before getting out of the seat he was in, stalking toward me with determination.

"What are you doing?" I ask, but he smirks like I should know what's about to happen.

"I'm going to see how it looks, so unless you tell me you don't want me to, I'm going to wrap my fingers around your pretty neck, sweetheart."

I let out a breathless laugh and back away from him until one of the walls of the studio touches my back.

"Do it."

His hand wraps around my throat without hesitation. My eyes flutter shut at the slight pressure he puts on each side of my throat.

"Yes, this is perfect," he says, applying a bit more pressure.

A small moan escapes me, and I open my eyes just in time to see Leonard biting his lip as he stares at his hand. He lowers it, admiring the way it looks as he grabs my tit, kneading it a little as he groans.

"Fuck yeah," he mutters to himself, dragging his hand even lower. "I wonder how perfect it'll look when I cup your pretty pussy. Can I try, sweetheart?"

"Yes," I reply, sucking in a breath to keep from moaning again when his hand moves between my legs, cupping my pussy over my clothes.

"I should have gotten this years ago," Leonard says right before he presses his mouth on mine and brings his hand back to my throat. He swipes his tongue over my bottom lip, so I part my lips for him. His taste surrounds me, and I sink into it, snaking my fingers around his wrist which is still near my throat.

"You should stop kissing me in case Giustina comes back inside," I warn him, but his kiss moves from my lips to my jaw.

"Tell me how and I will," he says, kissing me even harder.

"Leonard," I warn, but I don't tell him to stop nor do I push him away. It feels too good, having his hand wrapped around my throat and his mouth on mine.

It always feels so good.

"The sooner you get the tattoo, the sooner we can go home and finish this," I suggest, so Leonard breaks the kiss and turns toward where the front door is.

"Gi, I'm ready!" I burst into laughter at his enthusiasm, and he grins down at me in response.

Fuck, I love this man.

CHAPTER 17

Leonard

Chiara has done an outstanding job with the art gallery in Milan. I've been to this one when the other artist was still displaying their work, but what my wife has done is by far more captivating and creative.

Fine, I'm biased as hell, but even subjectively speaking, she outdid herself. It's so different from the one in London while still staying true to her style. One of the rooms in the immersive art gallery is a spin on a kid's ball pit, but every single ball is blue and some are hanging from the ceiling as if they're falling into the pit below. Another room plays with light. Another allows visitors to pick up some paint and draw on anything in the room. Starling had to ask Dino for permission, and he only agreed when she promised him it'd be water-removable paint.

"*Figlia*," Starling's mamma starts but finishes the sentence in Italian. She speaks too quickly for my brain to understand. I've been trying to learn Italian, but I'm picking it up very slowly.

"She told her what a wonderful job she's done here," Chiara's nonna says, so I turn toward her and offer her my arm so we can walk through the art gallery and make our way over to her granddaughter and daughter.

"She truly did," I reply, catching the way Nonna smiles at me.

"You look as in love with Chiara as you did when you first came to my house all those years ago. The honeymoon phase hasn't worn off, has it?" I shake my head and manage a smile for the woman who's become like my grandmother, too.

"Not even a little. If anything, I fall more in love with her every single time she gives me one of her smiles," I admit.

"Good. My *tesoro* deserves nothing less."

"I agree."

She shoots me another smile before adding, "She told me you two have decided to try and have a kid. How do you feel about that?"

"Excited? Anxious? Scared? All of the above?" I almost laugh. "Right now, I think I'm mostly nervous. We've been trying for almost a year without any luck." I recently went to the doctor to check if everything's alright with my sperm too, but she told me all is well. So, I'm getting extremely nervous.

"Sometimes it takes a while. Guilia's father and I were trying to get pregnant with her for almost two years. Then, one day, it happened. Your child will appear when they are ready and not a day before. Be patient."

Her reassurance settles me a little, so I place an arm around her and hug her to my side. She hugs me back before we keep walking.

Once we're in front of Guilia and Chiara, Nonna starts talking to them in Italian. Again, it's too fast for me to understand, but I enjoy listening to them anyway. My eyes scan the room once more, taking in my little demon's brilliant work.

Smart, creative, kind, beautiful beyond measure, and sassy as hell.

I really am the luckiest man alive.

"You have another gallery to fill with your ideas in Amsterdam, right?" Guilia asks her daughter, who nods.

"I have until December to finish it."

December.

Which is only two months away.

Two months until the end of the F1 season, too.

"That's not a lot of time! Do you know what kind of exhibits you would like to have there?" Nonna asks, concern laced in her words.

"I think I'll combine the ones I have here with some of the ones I have in London. It'll be similar, yet different enough not to disappoint people," Chiara explains, and I'm so proud of her for having thought this through so well, I could kiss her. I know she doesn't like the business end of this as much as the creative, but she's bloody good at both. "Plus, if I need more time, I'll ask Dino for more time. He's too scared of Leonard to deny me anything at this point." Starling's eyes sparkle with mischief as all three women suddenly look at me.

"What?" I ask.

"What did you do to him?" Nonna asks, and Guilia nods like she would love to know the answer to that question as well.

"I may or may not have threatened to bring him lots of pain in some very specific ways," I reply with a shrug, making my wife grin at me.

"I believe his words were, 'I swear I'll take that sign behind me that says 'Meteorite' and I'll hit you over the head with it for what you did to my wife.'" All three women start chuckling, causing heat to rush into my cheeks.

"You are quite a possessive man, aren't you?" Guilia says, so I rub my hand with my newest tattoo over my cheek, showing off the word "mine."

"I have no idea what you're talking about," I lie, but we all know I'm full of shit. I am possessive and protective. I will not stand for anyone hurting my woman in any capacity, nor will I stand for any member of our family to be hurt.

"Sure you don't," Chiara says, pointing at the tattoo hiding under my shirt on my left pec.

At her name.

We're four races away from the end of the season. I snatched pole yesterday with Jonathan in second, one of the Hawk drivers in third, Adrian in fourth, and Gabriel in fifth. We're in Miami right now, and it's so hot, I started sweating before I even got into my car. Now that I'm warming up my tyres and charging my battery during the formation lap, beads of it start rolling down my temple.

Right as all twenty drivers are about to move into the tenth corner of the formation lap, an alligator appears in my line of vision. I slam on my brakes and swerve to the side, Jonathan and all the drivers behind me doing the same thing.

"There's a fucking alligator on the track, Riley!" I say, my breath *whooshing* out of me.

"What do you mean?" they ask in response, and I shake my head.

"Exactly what I just said. It's not big. I think it's still a baby, and it's in danger. It needs to be removed," I say, checking my left mirror to see if it's still there or if one of the drivers hurt it by accident.

I don't see anything.

"Copy. Will inform the FIA."

Several moments later, after all the drivers have made their way back to their places on the starting grid, Riley tells me they need another moment. I don't blame them. I wouldn't even know where to begin removing an alligator from the track without accidentally hurting it or it killing me.

"This won't be good for the tyre temperature. We'll have no grip the longer we stay here without moving, without the tyre warmers on," I tell Riley.

"Agreed. I'll let Robert know."

Under these circumstances, the team principals can request to have another formation lap, but the FIA is the one to ultimately decide whether to grant this request or not. It also depends on how long we're standing until they've removed the animal. This isn't the first time something like this has happened. Usually, it's birds or once there was a honey badger in the middle of the way. It took forever to get it to safety because it kept running back and forth between the marshals, almost like it was playing with them.

It was hilarious.

This is not even a little funny. I'm worried about every member that has to be near the alligator. That might partially be because they are one of those animals I'd never want to encounter in real life. It's why I didn't go to any of the lakes or rivers here in Miami.

"They're still working on it, so you'll get another formation lap," Riley says a moment later, so I deflate a little in my seat.

Jonathan and I are merely twenty-five points apart. If for some reason, I DNF in any of the upcoming races and he comes in first, the gap between us will be closed entirely. No more gap. No more advantage. It'll be a battle.

I wish I could have already won the championship. I wish it would have been that simple, but, of course, it hasn't been.

"I thought you'd like to know that Adrian was on his radio and said, 'I didn't know we had another driver starting today. Someone get her a racing suit and helmet.'" I snort and shake my head.

Idiot.

"Thanks for sharing, Riley," I reply, shifting in my seat when I feel my left arse cheek go a little numb.

I hate sitting in the car without racing, especially once the adrenaline leaves. It's an effort to call it back, to put my mind back into racing mode.

"Alligator has been removed. Wait for the light to allow you to take another formation lap."

I do as I'm told, patiently waiting for the light before starting my car and making my way around the track again. The grip on my tyres is horrible, so I swerve from side to side, hoping it will get more heat into them.

My heart is finally pumping adrenaline back through my veins by the time we're all at the starting grid again. My hands flex around the steering wheel. My body stiffens in anticipation. I take a deep breath, thinking in my head, "I love you, little demon," a habit I've had since I fainted at the Qatar Grand Prix.

Just in case anything happens.

I text her, too, but it never feels like enough when she isn't here.

"Don't forget to downshift earlier to avoid running off the track in the corners," Riley reminds me right before the first light appears above me.

One by one, until they're all lit up, then vanish seconds later. I shift into gear and press down on the throttle. Jonathan's car appears right beside me as we move into the first corner, but, even though I brake, even though I slow down early enough, my car keeps moving until I'm in the gravel. It spins and only then do I notice the young Hawke driver, who was in third, following me straight into the barriers.

Fucking jerk ran right into me.

And ended my race before I could even make it to the second corner.

Jonathan leads the race now, and if he finishes first, the gap between us will be closed. If he gets the fastest lap too, he'll be a point ahead of me.

I slam my hands against the steering wheel and scream until my vocal cords give out.

But it's useless because Jonathan wins the race anyway.

He gets the fastest lap.

He leads the championship, and I only have three races left to make sure he doesn't fucking win it.

CHAPTER 18

Chiara

After Leonard's DNF in Miami, he came home, flopped onto the couch, and screamed into the pillow. I stood next to him with my arms crossed and a smile on my face because, as much as it pained me for him to miss out on winning that race, it'll never not amuse me when my grumpy, broody husband does something so out of character.

He's since won another race, but Jonathan came in second, which means they're only seven points apart now. Leonard is leading again, but I know he's having a hard time trying to stay positive. So, his way of cheering himself up—so he wouldn't be such a downer, his words, not mine—was to bring us to our island for a few days before he has to head back to work. Before I have to go back and finish my work at the gallery in Amsterdam as well.

For now, I'm enjoying the way the sun heats my skin. I'm enjoying the vacation, being away from our responsibilities for a few days. But I'm enjoying the book I'm reading even more, especially the way the main character is currently getting fucked in every position she's ever dreamed of.

My eyes shift to my husband, just like they always do when I read something that turns me on. I watch him stroll out of the water, drops of it running down his magnificent, tattooed chest. The outline of his impressive cock in his bathing suit captures all of my attention, and I watch his muscles flex with every move shamelessly.

His eyes are on me, like they always are, as he makes his way over to me.

My bottom lip slips between my teeth and, before I can think better of it, I slip my hands behind my back and undo the knot of my bikini top. It falls into the sand, followed a moment later by my bikini bottoms.

What's a private beach for if not to seduce your husband?

"Chiara Tick," he warns, but he's between my legs within a second. Water drips all over my body, the drops cool against my hot skin.

"Leonard Tick," I reply, running my nails over his abs. He leans down to kiss the inside of my left thigh, his attention shifting to my pussy.

"What have you been reading, sweetheart? What has you dripping wet?" He runs a single finger over my clit before dipping it inside of me and curling it to play with my G-spot. My back arches, a moan rushing out of me as pleasure consumes me.

"They played with overstimulation," I manage to explain right as he circles my clit.

"Do you want me to do that to you, baby? Do you want me to make you come over and over until you scream? Is that why you took your bikini off and spread your legs for me? Hmmm?" he asks, wrapping his tattooed hand around my throat.

"Yes." His mouth crashes onto mine and his fingers thrust back inside of me. "But I want you to use your cock. Let's see how often you can make me orgasm before you come, too," I say against his lips, bringing a confident smile to his face.

"You expect me to last when you're here, naked and clawing at my chest to get me closer? With your perfect breasts and heavenly pussy? And that smile, Chiara. Your smile is my biggest weakness of all." He bites down on my bottom lip, his fingers flexing on each side of my throat.

"Yes, I expect you to last."

Leonard lets out a low groan before slipping his finger out of me, grabbing my hips, and pulling me down until my back is flat against the towel. He catches the back of my head to keep it from slamming against the ground as he maneuvers me around until he's happy with my position. He spreads my legs wider, then slides down his swim trunks, exposing his hard cock.

My mouth waters at the sight of it.

"I love your cock," I say as I reach out to stroke it. Leonard's eyes flutter shut at the sensation, his fingers digging into my legs. "I love how good you make me feel with it," I add, circling my thumb over his tip.

"Fuuuuck, Chiara, you need to stop, please, sweetheart. Otherwise, I won't be able to make you come even once," he pleads, so I let go of him, placing my hands on his hips and sliding them onto his ass to grab it.

"I also love your ass. It's so round and firm," I swoon because he always makes me feel so good about my body, about me. It needs to be reciprocated; it cannot be one-sided. Not in a relationship and especially not in a marriage. I want Leonard to feel desirable. I want him to know how sexy I think he is. I want him to know everything.

"You make me a very weak man, sweetheart." He rubs his cock over my clit as he says it, lust clouding his eyes. "By the time we're done, you won't be able to walk for a few days without your legs shaking. You'll feel me with every step." He leans down to kiss me right as he aligns himself with my entrance, sinking deep inside me.

"Leonard," I whimper, clenching around his cock. I roll my hips in search of friction, so he places his thumb on my clit and rubs.

"That's it, sweetheart. Squeeze my cock. Chase your pleasure," he praises, slipping out just to drive back into me with so much force, I scream in pleasure.

His free hand moves onto my breast, squeezing my nipple between his fingers until another bolt of pleasure shoots down my spine.

His thrusts combined with the circles he rubs on my clit and the gentle pressure and pain originating from where he's pinching my nipple has my stomach tensing.

He drives into me harder and faster until all that escapes my lips are moans of pleasure.

"Fuck, Leonard, oh my God. I'm gonna come," I cry out, my entire body shaking right as my orgasm washes through me, blindsiding me.

Leonard slows his thrusts, watching me come down from my high with a smug smirk.

"That's one," he says, pulling out of me just long enough to rub his cock over my clit again.

My entire body trembles, too sensitive from the first orgasm.

"Remember, either tap me on the forehead or tell me to stop when you're done." I nod in response, a smile of pleasure finding its way onto my lips.

He gives me another moment while I run my fingers over my name where it's tattooed on his left pec. My eyes study his brown ones before admiring his beautiful dark skin, then his full lips. Noticing where my attention has drifted, he kisses me thoroughly, his fingers carefully running over my pussy. A second later, he flips me around so I'm on my stomach, his dick slipping back inside without hesitation. His hand moves between my body and the towel, finding my clit.

"Yes, yes, yes!" I chant with every thrust, with every time I grind against his hand, too.

"You feel so fucking good, sweetheart. I won't last long," he says, angling my hips a little to find that sweet spot inside of me.

Minutes later, I'm screaming through another orgasm, pushing back against him to chase my pleasure for as long as I can.

His full weight appears against my backside as he leans down to whisper, "That's two," into my ear.

He cheats for the third orgasm when he goes down on me and makes me come on his mouth, grinding against his face.

"You know what drives me wild, Chiara?" he asks, running his hands all over my body.

"Tell me," I reply with a breathless laugh.

"When you taste like me right here..." He trails off and runs his tongue down my pussy again.

Leonard kisses up my body, wrapping his lips around each of my nipples to play with them. I pull on his curls, arching my back and shoving my tit further into his mouth.

"One more, Champ, and this time, I want you to come inside of me."

"Anything you want, my wife."

His pace is perfect, his thrusts precise and calculated, designed solely to make me come as quickly as possible because we both know he can't last much longer. He hasn't felt any release since we started fucking who-knows how long ago, and he's desperate to come. So, he fucks me harder and faster, chasing his pleasure as he moans and groans over and over. A whimper even escapes him as I clench my walls around his cock, making his entire body tremble.

"Fuck, sweetheart."

He drives into me again, and I repeat that same movement, sending him straight over the edge. Leonard calls out my name, rolling his hips as he comes inside of me. I follow him, pushing myself off him a little and then moving back toward him to bounce on his cock. He collapses on top of me moments later, his skin slick with sweat and his heart racing as quickly as mine.

I wrap my legs around his waist, keeping him buried deep inside me. They already feel sore, trembling a little as I try to flex them around my husband.

"I think this is the only thing we should be doing from now on. Just make love. Every minute of every day," he says, and I snort at his words.

Sadness replaces my amusement.

"Maybe then I'd finally get pregnant," I mumble, hating myself for ruining the moment but also wanting to share how I'm feeling. "I know we said we'd adopt if I couldn't get pregnant, but I did like the idea of a mini Leonard running around our apartment."

"I know, Chiara. I want a mini you as well, but I'll love any kid we bring into our lives. Adopted or biological." He rubs his nose over my chest, then looks up to smile at me. "But we're not done trying yet, and I have a good feeling it'll happen soon."

He kisses me, and I sink into the feeling, letting his hopefulness wash through me.

CHAPTER 19

Leonard

L ast race.

My last race with Grenzenlos.

My last race fighting for a championship.

My last race with so much pressure on my back.

Quinn is helping me warm up, doing her best trying to settle my nerves. She keeps slapping my arms when she notices my thoughts drifting to worst-case scenarios. If I get first place, I win. If I get second place and Jonathan first, I win. If he's first and I come in third... I lose. If I DNF, I obviously lose, and that fucking Hawke driver is starting in third again, right behind me. If he collides with me again, that's it. I'm done.

My last chance for a third championship will have slipped through my hands.

Everything's on the line today, and I can't make a single mistake.

"Okay, we have to find a way to get you out of your head. You're more likely to make a mistake when you're worrying about making a mistake than if you merely go into this with confidence. You need to stop worrying. How do we do that?" Quinn asks, tapping her index finger against her arm where it's crossed in front of her chest.

"I don't know. Do you have any good news I can fixate on?" I say with a humourless laugh that sounds more like a breathless wheeze.

"My dad had his annual checkup a few weeks ago. Everything looks great," she offers, but I merely nod.

"As awesome as that is, it's not going to be enough to stop me from spiralling."

Quinn's lips seal shut as she thinks about what to tell me. My thoughts drift to my wife at the same moment she steps into the room, peeking her head through the door first to see if she's intruding.

"Come here, sweetheart," I say without hesitation, holding out my hands for her because there is nothing better than having her comfort while I'm freaking out.

"What's going on?" she asks, placing her hands on my chest where my fireproofs cover me.

"Quinn and I are trying to get me out of my head, but the only good news she had for me isn't enough to do that," I explain and shoot her a teasing scowl. My best friend flips me off without hesitation while Chiara chuckles.

"Have you spoken to Adrian? I heard he's got some news about what team he'll be racing for next season," Chiara suggests, running her hands further up my body to snake her fingers around my neck.

"He already told me he's going to Velocità Rossa a few days ago. And Robert told me they retracted their offer after what happened in Italy." Where Adrian wrecked his car on a mistake that shouldn't happen to a seasoned driver, according to my team principal. But it wasn't entirely his fault either, and no one can expect a driver to be perfect all the time. There's a difference between a driver always making a mistake and a driver making one every once in a blue moon like Adrian.

"What about Jack and Stu? Maybe little Hudson has said his first word," she suggests with a little smile. There's something mischievous in her gaze, and I furrow my brows as I study it.

"Stop tormenting the man, would you?" Quinn says, grinning like she knows something I should know, too. "I'll give you two a moment." My best friend leaves without another word, but my attention is on my wife.

"What news? Chiara. Tell me. What news?" Tears shoot into her eyes, making some shoot into mine.

"You know how I've been at the art gallery in Amsterdam for the last two weeks?" She went there almost immediately after we got back from our vacation, so I nod several times, hope still blooming in my chest. "Well, a week ago or so, I should have gotten my period." She pauses as tears drop down her cheeks. "But I didn't. So, this morning, I took a test. Quinn caught me crying in the bathroom. Crying because of this," she says and pulls out a pregnancy test.

It reads, "positive."

I drop to my knees without meaning to, taking her with me. My arms fling around her, pulling her against me until there's no more space between us. Then, I cry. I cry so hard, and Chiara cries, too. We're both sobbing because we've been trying for so long. This is what we wanted for even longer.

And it's finally happening.

"Please tell me this is real, sweetheart," I beg, my entire body shaking.

"It's real, *amore*. I'm pregnant," she says and laughs, clinging to me. More tears escape my eyes as I rock us back and forth, the overload of joy taking hold of every part of my body. "We're gonna have a baby," she adds, a sob shaking her chest.

"We're having a baby," I repeat, still in disbelief. "Fuck, I don't even need the championship anymore. This is the best news I could have gotten today," I say, trying to lighten the mood even if deep down, that's how I really feel.

I still want the title, but I'm not as stressed about it anymore.

Because I already got a way better one.

"I'm going to be a dad again."

One light.

Two.

Three.

Four.

Five.

I hold my breath.

Wait.

Exhale as they all vanish.

My car speeds into the first corner. I brake perfectly on time, Jonathan right behind me as he tries to fight me for first place. I won't let him overtake me. This is my race. This is *my* third title. I have a wife to make proud, a Nonna and Mamma, too. They're both here, watching and probably praying for me. I can't disappoint them. When I tell my kid about this season, I will tell them I won. I will share my success with them and inspire them to chase whatever dream they have.

My muscles tense as the G-force hits my body, making sweat drip down my spine. Jonathan's car slips beside mine as we head into the fifth corner, but I defend well, keeping my position. My body is thrown from side to side, so I tense even more, trying to keep from bouncing in my seat.

Fun fact about F1 car seats, they're fucking uncomfortable, even if they're molded to perfectly fit your arse and back.

"Leonard, you have to push. Create a gap," Riley says, and I almost groan.

"What the bloody hell do you think I'm doing?" I say, breathless all over again. It's different from earlier but just as unpleasant.

The next five laps are difficult, to say the least. Jonathan fights me at every corner, at every straight, using his DRS advantage once it's enabled. Fortunately for me, he gets told to manage his tyres when he doesn't overtake me by lap six, and I let out a breath of relief. Defending and attacking are even more straining on the body than normal racing.

Entirely out of breath, I create a gap between Jonathan and me, driving away at the front as much as possible. This gap will be important when we get to the first pitstop of the race.

"Good pace, keep it up," Riley says before telling me my sector times and their prediction of how big the gap will be between Jonathan and me in ten laps. If both of us continue this way, that is.

"Riley, it feels like something's loose under the car," I say once we hit lap fifteen, the car vibrating more than usual when I take the curb.

"Checking," is their only reply.

Fuck.

If something's wrong with the car, I'm done.

Fuck, fuck.

The silence over the radio is tormenting. With every second Riley doesn't tell me what's wrong with the car, I get more nervous. It's unsettling to have so much to lose and being entirely powerless over the performance of the car.

If it fails me, there's nothing I can do to change it.

Fuck, fuck, fuck.

"Riley, I'm going to need an answer."

"Still checking."

I bite back a groan of frustration.

The rattling I feel on the curbs keeps happening as I complete two more laps. The gap between Jonathan and me is big enough now that when I check my mirrors he's quite far behind. It's the only thing assuring me that whatever is happening can't be bad enough to slow me down.

"Riley," I say right as I enter lap eighteen.

"We can't find anything, Leonard. Just keep driving. It's nothing to worry about," they promise me. "You can push your tyres a bit more, too. Use them before we have our first pitstop," Riley adds, and I take a deep breath to concentrate.

I didn't use to have so many doubts and worries. I was confident. When I led a championship, I won it. After what happened last season, I've become a master overthinker when it comes to racing. It's incredibly frustrating.

"Box, box," Riley says laps later, so I bring my car into the pits, slowing to the designated speed as I move to where my crew is waiting with fresh tyres.

Everything goes smoothly, but when I get the green light to be released, I almost crash into Adrian as he makes his way to his crew. I slam on my brakes and he swerves to the side to avoid colliding.

"What the fuck was that Riley? Why did they give me the green light if it wasn't safe to be released?" My voice is full of rage.

This will cost us.

This will end in a penalty.

This—

I scream into my helmet.

"I'm sorry, Leonard," is their only response, which doesn't help at all. It's neither an explanation nor can it undo what just happened.

"Just tell me when we get a penalty."

There's nothing I can do but wait and see what the FIA will do. There *will* be a penalty, they have to give me one, it's part of the rules. But I hope it's not a drastic one.

I warm my tyres before picking up speed to chase down Jonathan in first place. He has yet to pit, which means the more I can close the time gap between us, the bigger it'll be when I'm back in first and he's second.

I'm given a five-second penalty for my unsafe release, one I can either serve when I go in for my second pitstop, or it can be added onto my time at the end of the race.

"What's the plan?" I ask Riley, uncertainty rolling through me. I don't know what the better option is.

"If you serve it during the pitstop, Adrian will definitely overtake you. It would be risky, but we can let it be added at the end. You'll just have to make the gap bigger than five seconds between you and Adrian in third place."

So far, I've only been able to get about four and a half seconds on Adrian. Jonathan is about two seconds behind me.

"Okay, I'll serve it during the pitstop. I just have to chase Adrian down after." Easy, at least, I hope it'll be.

By the time my second pitstop comes around, Adrian has already pitted and so has Jonathan. I've accepted that I won't win this race, but I'll settle for second. Second will still get me the title if Jonathan wins.

"Make sure I have a safe release," I scold right as I enter the pits.

"Copy." I can hear them cringing in their voice, but until I've won the championship, I'm going to be a little mad.

My pitstop goes as smoothly as possible, relatively quickly, too. I'm in third place then, a few seconds behind Adrian.

Time to chase my friend.

Within twelve laps, I'm close enough to activate my DRS to gain a speed advantage. The end of the race draws nearer and nearer, but I can't panic yet. Five laps is enough time to overtake him. The Spark isn't fast enough on this track to hold me off forever.

Four laps and I've gotten closer.

Three laps, and I attempt an overtake that doesn't stick.

Two laps, and—

I watch Jonathan move into the third corner, his car spinning in circles. Adrian and I shoot past him before he can recover. A yellow flag is waved in the sector where it happened, according to Riley, but once Jonathan has regained control of his car, the sector goes green again. But Jonathan is in tenth now.

One lap, and I stop fighting Adrian to spare my tyres. To keep from making an unnecessary mistake that could end my race.

The last corner appears in my line of vision, then the finish line.

A breath later, I'm the Champion of the World.

Fireworks explode in the sky. The crowd bursts into cheers. My heart races as another wave of adrenaline ripples through my chest.

I did it.

I got my third championship title.

I'm World Champion again.

I pinch my leg just to make sure this isn't a dream, and then Riley's voice rushes through my earpiece and I *know* this isn't a dream.

"You got it! You won! Congratulations, mate. This is so well deserved," they say, cheering me on as I drive the car around the track for the cool-down lap, waving at all my fans and everyone else who's screaming my name.

"FUCK YEAH!" I scream over the radio, tears filling my eyes.

As soon as my car is parked at the second place sign, I jump out of it, rushing toward Chiara. I wrap my arms around her without hesitation, pulling her to my chest by cupping the back of her head and placing a hand on her lower back.

"I'm so proud of you," she says, hugging me back just as hard.

"I love you so much. I love you. I love you." I repeat the same words over and over, sliding a hand over her stomach because I love our baby so much already, too. "This one is for both of you," I tell Chiara, who kisses the space on my helmet where it covers my mouth.

"I love you, Champ." I hug her again, unable to let go because she settles me. She places the ground under my feet again.

She makes everything feel less like a fantasy, even though she's my biggest dream.

CHAPTER 20
Chiara

"Whoever said pregnancy was a wonderful experience can go throw themselves off a fucking cliff. Nothing about this experience is *wonderful*." Scarlette smiles at me, placing a hand on my shoulder in comfort.

"And imagine, all of that just to have a crying, screaming baby that keeps you from getting any sleep for the first three or seven years. I don't really know how kids work," she admits before bursting into laughter at my scowl. "I'm sorry. That's not helpful, is it?" she asks, squeezing my shoulder.

"Not in the slightest," I reply, still glaring at her.

"Julián and I both agreed having a kid isn't for us, so I can't even say one day I'll understand," she says with a shrug.

"Honestly? Good choice," I say, trying to find any sitting position that makes me feel comfortable.

It always feels like I have to pee because my precious little baby is pressing on my bladder all the fucking time. My ankles are swollen, my back hurts, and I cry every few hours now because of hormones. I saw a squirrel cross the street yesterday and was so worried, I started sobbing to Leonard about how dangerous it is for them to live because of us humans. He tried his best to comfort me and be understanding, but I could tell he had no idea how to make me feel better.

"Seeing how miserable you are, I'd definitely say I made the right choice," Scarlette agrees, and I nudge her side, making her burst into laughter.

"Only another month. I can make it another month, hopefully without accidentally peeing my pants," I say, rubbing my hands over my swollen belly as worry consumes me because *what the fuck do I do if that actually happens?*

"How's work going?" Scar asks me, my concern probably evident on my face if she's switching the topic.

"Very good. My other two art galleries opened about half a year ago, and business is great. Leonard and I have even discussed moving to Monaco to open an art gallery there. More money," I explain with a sly smile.

"That's a good idea. We've also been thinking about moving to Europe, but we're not sure where yet. My best friend and her husband want to follow us, so we've been having a hard time figuring out a place we'll all like." She laughs, ever the sunshine.

"Well, your husband races for MotoGP and you're a soon-to-be F1 race engineer. Anywhere in Europe will be good for you, honestly." Scarlette nods, a thoughtful expression slipping onto her face.

She opens her mouth to reply when Valentina Romana, current reserve driver for Velocità Rossa and future Alfa Adrenalina driver, steps into the room. Leonard and Julián interrupt their conversation to greet her, the Puerto Rican with a stiff nod and my husband with a "hey, kiddo." Adrian, on the other hand, welcomes his sister by wrapping an arm around her shoulders and pressing a very wet kiss to her temple.

"Gross," she mutters and wipes it away, but the smile on her face betrays her. She loves her brother, probably more than anything, and it shows.

Well, more than almost anything.

But we don't talk about Gabriel right now.

That *stronzo* can throw himself off the same cliff as the people who lied about pregnancy.

"Hey, Val. Come sit with us," Scar says, her smile bright and inviting. The racecar driver returns it, but it doesn't reach her tired eyes.

Valentina is beautiful beyond question. She has curly, dirty-blonde hair that falls down her back. Her eyes are bright, a combination of green, blue, and brown. She's curvy and trained, and her smile is magical, even when she only half means it. While she walks with confidence and grace, I notice the way her hands shake a little. The way she focuses on her feet, most likely to make sure she doesn't stumble or trip over them.

"Hi," she says, lifting her fingers to tuck a few strands of hair behind her left ear. "Thank you again for coming to watch me test drive my brother's F1 car today. It made today very special." Valentina settles down beside Scarlette, and her future race engineer places a hand on top of hers to squeeze it.

"It's our pleasure. We want to support you as much as we can," Scarlette replies, tilting her head my way and making her dark, wavy hair bounce with the movement. "Isn't that right, Chiara?"

"Of course it is, but I will hold you accountable for the little incident I had earlier," I tell Valentina, leaning back in my chair and rubbing my sore belly again. The stretch marks I had before getting pregnant have become more visible and also more sensitive.

Then again, all of me feels sensitive right now.

"What incident?" Valentina asks, leaning forward to give me her full attention.

"I was so excited about the lap times you were setting, I forgot to go to the bathroom and almost peed myself," I explain, watching a bigger smile cover her lips, one that reaches her eyes, too.

I was hoping for this reaction. It's the only reason I told her this story.

"It was impressive, wasn't it?" she asks, pride making her sit a bit straighter.

"Faster than your brother," Scarlette mumbles, making sure Adrian doesn't hear her.

"I *am* faster than my brother," Valentina says, but she projects her voice to ensure her brother hears every word. She throws him a challenging look, but he merely raises his pinky at her in response.

She asks me about my art galleries, too, before we fall into a comfortable silence. My eyes shift to my husband, who's scowling at whatever Adrian's showing him and Julián on his phone. When I look at Valentina again, I notice she's taken off her necklace and is staring at it, twisting the charm between her fingers.

"Do you want to talk about it? I know it must be difficult only having Mr. Anti-Relationship to turn to," I say, tilting my head to study her reaction. Her light eyes fixate on my face, tracing my features as they fill with tears. She swallows and they're gone, but I know she's been crying. Anyone could see it in the redness and puffiness around her eyes, how bloodshot they are.

"I love him so much, which is the unfairest part of all. He left. I shouldn't love him because of it, but I cannot stop. I cannot will myself to forget how it felt when he kissed me. Touched me. Told me he loved me. I can't delete every memory, but they're the ones inflicting the pain I can't breathe past."

The tears return, but this time, they fall down her cheeks. She wipes them away, taking a deep breath.

"I wanted a future with him, *everything* with him. How do I move on from that?" she asks, looking every bit as helpless as I'd expect anyone would feel this shortly after a big breakup.

"Fuck him," is the first thing that comes out of my mouth. "Fuck him for ever making you feel this way. Fuck him for leaving you when times got hard. Fuck him for being a coward. No matter his intentions, what he did was wrong," I add, but Scarlette presses her lips into a thin line, obviously disagreeing.

"While I agree that he went about it the wrong way, I'm sure the reason he left isn't rooted in the desire to break up with you. I know he loves you. He showed the entire world what you mean to him, so much so that when people spoke about him, your name followed shortly after. Once he figures himself out, he'll come back to you, and if you still want him, I'm sure you can work it out."

The same disagreeing look that covered her face after my rant now covers mine. Only I feel the way my features contort into disgust as well.

"You better make him drop to his fucking knees and beg when he comes back," I say, cocking an irritated eyebrow. If I were Valentina, I would punch Gabriel in the face, but she's a better, less violent person than me, so she won't.

She really should, though.

"You two are like an angel and devil on my shoulders," Valentina replies, laughing a little. I exchange a look with Scarlette, smirking at the accuracy of that comparison.

"Right after I push this baby out of me, I'm available to be hired for torture again, if you want to get some revenge on him," I offer with a teasing smile, making her burst into laughter.

"No, if anyone punishes that man for his stupid actions, it'll be me."

"Atta girl," I praise, watching her cheeks go red as she keeps smiling.

"Thank you for being here for me, for listening. It means a lot."

"Don't mention it, *bella*."

Scarlette and Valentina fall into a conversation about racing while I look at my husband, desperately needing his help. Now that my stomach is the size of a very large pumpkin, getting up has become a lot more difficult. It takes effort, so, usually, he helps me stand. I won't ask anyone else because I don't *like* asking for help, but my husband should just know. Most of the time, it's like he can sense it. I don't know if my expressions are so easily readable for him or if he has developed a sixth sense.

Either way, I'm grateful when his eyes drift to me. He notices the look I'm giving him and instantly jumps to his feet. He's in front of me seconds later, his hands reaching for me to help me stand.

"Thank you," I whisper, so he catches my lips in a sweet kiss, smiling against them.

"Anything for you two," he replies, grabbing my hand to walk with me to the bathroom.

"Have you spoken to Valentina about 'Kids Like Us' again?" I ask.

Leonard came up with the title not long after he started mentoring Valentina when she joined Velocità Rossa's driver academy. He discussed her becoming his business partner a few weeks ago, and she agreed, which means they have a lot of work to do now. Investors to find. People to convince of their idea.

"No, I wanted to give her time during the summer break to focus on test driving, but I will speak to her as soon as the season restarts," he replies, tilting his head my way to press his lips against my temple. My eyes flutter shut at the sweet gesture for a moment, enjoying the way a single kiss can send warmth through my chest.

"I can't wait to go home and get back to Benzie again," I admit as we stop in front of the washroom.

"I know, sweetheart. Me neither." I look up into his warm brown eyes, stepping toward him to wrap my arms around his neck. My belly presses against his, making it difficult to pull him close and kiss him. But he meets me halfway.

He cups my cheeks and kisses me so hard, it serves as a reminder of how much he loves me.

How much he worships me.

How grateful he is I'm growing a life inside of me so we can expand our family.

From getting me my late-night cravings to helping me with my morning sickness to having even more patience than usual, Leonard has done it all. He's been perfect throughout this whole pregnancy, and it's beyond annoying that I can never get upset with him because he does *everything* for me.

Without a single complaint.

No one should ever settle for less than the treatment my husband gives me.

CHAPTER 21
Leonard

The sound of Starling's scream ripples through my ear, sending a wave of pain through my system.

"Breathe, sweetheart. Please, you need to breathe." I run a hand over her forehead, but she swats it away and glares at me.

"Don't touch me right now," she growls, and I retract my hand instantly. She confuses me when she grabs it a second later, squeezing my fingers together as she attempts to breathe through another contraction.

"What can I do to help you?" I've never felt so useless and powerless in my life.

"Get me the fucking drugs, Leonard Tick. Any they have to offer. I will not push this child out of me without them," she says.

Uh oh, whenever she uses my full name in this tone, I'm in trouble.

I run out of the room, tracking down Chiara's midwife. After telling her my wife's request, she disappears down the hall, leaving me to try and catch my breath. Ever since her contractions started a few hours ago, I've been breathless. Afraid. Freaking out. Something beyond nervous and paranoid.

"I'm here. Your handsome emotional support man is finally here. I came as quickly as my plane could fly. You're lucky I was already in Scotland for some sightseeing," he says, his smile easy and his gaze full of reassurance and comfort that he's here for anything we need.

I don't know what comes over me. Whether it's having been in panic mode for so long or some other force, but I fling my arms around him, hugging him to my chest.

Adrian goes unnaturally stiff.

"What the fuck is happening? They didn't teach this in the Leonard Tick crash course I took," he says, and I let out a small chuckle.

He goes even stiffer.

"Thank you for being here, kiddo," I mumble as I step out of the hug, his eyes comically wide. "Means a lot," I add, squeezing his shoulder.

"Well, of course. If the baby comes out looking like me instead of you, I figured it'd be best if I explained what happened to your face," he teases, so I swat him upside the back of his head. "What? I can't handle feelings, so I use humour to deflect. You just made me feel a lot of things!" he explains, and I chuckle again.

It's difficult to keep up my grumpy, cold façade when I'm so fucking scared of something going wrong.

"I'm terrified." The words slip out before I can stop them. And honestly, I don't want to stop them.

"Everything will be okay, Leonard, I promise," he says right as we stop outside of Chiara's room. "Chiara is one of the strongest people in the world, and if your baby is as stubborn as you and her, they'll be just fine."

Although he has no possible way of knowing, his reassurance settles me.

"Yeah, you're right," I say, laughing a little before adding, "I'll just have to find a way to get my wife to let me touch her again." Adrian bursts into laughter.

"Did she say that?" he asks, crossing his arms in front of his chest as he looks in the direction of the half-opened door.

"Yes, she did, and she meant it. You and your dick are never coming anywhere near me again, Leonard Tick. Mark my fucking words," my wife says. I cringe at Starling's words, rubbing the back of my neck as I stare at the ground.

We walk inside the room, both of us moving to stand by her sides.

"Can't say I blame you," I admit, and Adrian nods in agreement.

"Do you want mine instead?" Adrian asks, and my wife lets out a breathless laugh.

"I'm giving birth, and you're flirting with me?" If it didn't make her smile, I'd punch Adrian in the face for his question, but anything that distracts Chiara even slightly from the pain while we wait for the epidural is worth it.

I'll just kill him later.

"No better time than the present," he says and places a hand on the top of her head. When she doesn't swat it away, I frown.

"So, he gets to touch you?" The scowl that follows makes me shake a little.

"He didn't do this to me. *You* did. You and your massive penis." Adrian gives me an impressed smile.

"How massive?" he whispers to Chiara, who rearranges herself on the hospital bed to search for a more comfortable position.

"None of your bloody business," I say, but he merely cocks an amused brow at me.

"I wanna know if it's bigger than mine. Let me go get the ruler so we can measure and compare," he replies, making Chiara laugh again before she covers her ears with her hands.

"You're a child," she points out.

"Perhaps, but it made you laugh, so I'll gladly act like a child," he says with a wink, and I remember what he said to me not long ago.

"My whole life, I've always become whatever people needed me to be. A friend. A brother. A shoulder. An image. Anything to make them happy. Sometimes I wonder if I even remember who I am when I'm not any of these things."

I looked at him that day and understood him a little better than I had before.

"You're Adrian Romana. You are all of these things and more."

My response made him smile brighter than I'd ever seen before.

"I'll be outside if you need me. Unless you want me to stay instead of Leonard," he offers as he removes his hand from where he placed it on Chiara's shoulder a moment ago.

"Out," I demand, pointing at the door.

He gives me a cocky smile, then leaves after placing a soft kiss on Chiara's hand and saying, "You got this, Mamma. I believe in you."

I watch after him for a moment, mesmerized once more at the sheer purity of his heart, but Starling brings my attention back to her when she grabs my hand and places it on her cheek.

"I want your touch more than anyone else's." It's a reassurance I didn't know I needed until the words process in my brain. Her face contorts as another contraction brings pain to her entire body.

"I'm sorry you have to be the one to bear this pain alone, sweetheart. I'm so sorry I cannot take it from you. Because I would. In a heartbeat," I say, leaning down to kiss the top of her head.

"I know, *amore*," she says, her eyes closed when I step back again. "But I really need the epidural. I can't do this for much longer," she cries, tears streaming down her face. I wipe them away, promising that her midwife will be here soon.

I almost throw up and pass out when the midwife shows us the epidural.

Why the fuck is the tube so big?

Covering my mouth with my hand, I look at the ceiling while the midwife pushes the needle into my wife's spine. It takes a while to administer, then another while for it to set in, but Chiara almost gasps in relief when it does.

Her Mamma and Nonna appear a while later, waiting with my parents and siblings in the waiting room as well.

Chiara starts pushing soon after.

Every cry, every push, every contraction makes me want to burn the entire fucking world to the ground.

"Leonard," she cries, her grip on my hand tightening.

"I'm here, sweetheart. I'm here," I assure her, running a wet cloth across her forehead to remove the beads of sweat that have collected there.

"I'm so tired," she says after another contraction, another push.

"I know. Just a little longer, and we'll get to meet our baby. Don't you want to meet her?" Chiara nods, sitting upright a little more.

"Alright, Mrs. Tick, a few more pushes," her doctor says, and my wife nods eagerly.

Moments later, a scream fills the entire room. My heart stutters and stumbles at the sight of my daughter in Doctor Lucy's hands. I cut the umbilical cord, never looking away from my child as a feeling of pure awe settles everywhere inside of me.

When she's placed in Chiara's arms, I almost sink to my knees. I have an arm wrapped around my wife's head, my other hand reaching out to touch my daughter's tiny toes. Tears stream down Starling's face, and mine follow shortly after, dripping down my cheeks as I stare at the little baby who looks so much like her Mamma, she's beautiful. She has my nose from what I can tell, but that's it. The mouth, the ears, everything just reminds me of Chiara. God, I hope she'll have her eyes, too. My wife has the most beautiful eyes, and I want our daughter's to be the same.

"I hope she has your eyes," Chiara says, contradicting my thoughts. She trails a careful finger along our daughter's nose, more tears falling from her eyes.

"I was just thinking that I hope she has yours," I reply, smiling at Chiara.

"No, your eyes are my favorite. I want her to have yours," she says, tilting her head up to look at me. Our gazes meet right before I lean down to press a kiss to her lips.

"Thank you for making our dream come true. Thank you for being my wife. Thank you for being my everything and giving me everything." She kisses me longer and harder, but our moment is interrupted as Doctor Lucy tells us about how the placenta still needs to come out.

My daughter is taken away again to check if everything is alright while Chiara goes through the post-giving birth process.

I've been holding my daughter for a while. I have no idea how long, but Starling has been asleep for most of it, getting rest after *pushing a small human being out of her vagina.* She can have all the rest in the world. I'll take care of everything while she sleeps.

"We have to name her," my little demon says when she wakes up, interrupting my tracing my daughter's face with my gaze. She's so small, yet priceless.

She's a little wonder.

Our little wonder.

"Whatever you want to name her is fine with me. It'll be perfect," I say, pressing a kiss on my little girl's forehead.

"I've had a name in mind for a while, so I'm glad you feel this way," she says, sitting up in her bed to stretch her arms out, signaling for me to place our daughter in them.

"Tell me," I reply as soon as Chiara is holding her.

"Leonora." My wife looks up at me as she cradles our daughter's head. "Leonora Guilia Rena Tick," she says, incorporating my name as well as our mothers' names in it.

"We need to find a way to incorporate your name, too," I point out, crying again because this is by far the sweetest name and gesture.

"No, I think this is perfect. Plus, we don't want to give her too many names," my wife says with a grin, but I'm still crying. I'm swallowing a sob, fighting back the desire to break down and weep because this all feels like a dream I never want to wake up from.

My two perfect girls.

I will protect them with my life for as long as I breathe.

"I love you two so much," I blurt out, leaning down to kiss Chiara's forehead, then Leonora's.

Nothing will ever hurt them.

I will make sure of it.

And if I can't prevent it, you can be bloody sure I'll destroy whatever will have brought them pain.

CHAPTER 22
Chiara

Almost One Year Later

"I always knew he'd fall harder than everyone else," I tell Leonard as we watch Adrian hugging his girlfriend—Robert Fuchs' daughter, Nevaeh Fuchs—to his chest.

He presses a soft kiss to her lips, and she giggles in response, her cheeks flushing bright red. Adrian's smile is like bottled-up sunshine finally being released.

Because of her job, they've been keeping their relationship secret, but Leonard, me, Val, Gabriel, James, Scarlette, Julián, Cameron, and his boyfriend, Elijah, know. Which is why all of us are here tonight, celebrating Cameron's birthday. They trusted us with this secret, but even if they hadn't, it's clear as day that they're in love. Anyone could see it if they took more than a second to study the way they look at each other.

"Not harder than me," Leonard says next to me, Leonora sleeping on her daddy's lap. She's almost a year old, and I wish I knew where the time has gone because I'm not prepared for my baby to become a toddler already. Then a kindergartner. A school kid. I almost cry at the thought.

"I don't know, Champ. He hasn't taken his eyes off her longer than five seconds tonight. You've hardly looked at me," I tease, pretending to mean the words when I know full well they aren't true.

"Firstly, I look at you more in one night than an average person looks at their partner in their entire lives. Secondly, I've only looked away from you to look at our daughter. When he has a kid, it'll be the same for him. His attention eternally divided between his greatest treasures."

Leonard moves toward me to plant his lips on my cheek. I tilt my head at the last moment, meeting his kiss with my mouth. He smiles, deepening the kiss only long enough to leave my head spinning when he pulls back again.

"Hmmm," slips out of my mouth, my teeth sinking into my bottom lip as I enjoy the lingering taste of my husband on my tongue.

Benz barks up at me, the old girl still so full of energy. I lean forward to pet her, which she takes as an invitation to jump up onto the outdoor furniture Valentina and Gabriel have at their home. She licks my cheek, standing half on my thigh and half on the cushion of the sofa. I burst into laughter while Leonard and Leonora both look at us, our daughter now fully awake. I smile at her before Benz licks me again.

"Oh, wait, let me take a picture!" I hear someone call out.

Nevaeh appears in front of us with her camera, grinning so hard, her cheeks must hurt. She finds the right position to take a photo, and I hold Benz in place, nudging Leonard in the ribs to make sure I have his attention before I speak.

"Smile," I hiss through my teeth, already smiling.

He shifts Leonora around so she faces the camera.

"I don't smile," he responds.

"Smile, or we won't have sex tonight." It's a whisper, only loud enough for him to hear.

My husband has never smiled so hard in his life.

And I can't contain my laughter.

"Perfect," Nevaeh says after she took what feels like a hundred pictures.

She turns her camera for us to see, and once we've praised her on how wonderful they are, Adrian wraps his arms back around her, guiding her against his chest. He mumbles something into her ear that has her cheeks turning red. I smile at them before my gaze drifts back to Leonora and Leonard. My husband bounces our daughter on his thigh and she giggles and giggles and giggles like it's the funniest thing ever.

"I want to have another one," I blurt out, reaching out to grab our daughter's face between my hands. Her bright green eyes, a copy of mine, find me, making her smile.

Leonard cups my cheek and kisses me again.

"As many as you want," he says with a little smile.

Our daughter reaches for me, so I pick her up and hug her to my chest.

"Because it's you, me, and them, little demon. Forever."

"Forever," I echo, feeling his lips on mine again a second later.

Forever.

Sneak-Peek from Rush: Part One & Two

Chapter 1
Valentina

Spending fourteen hours on a flight with my brother while he snores into my ear is *not* fun. Adrian usually doesn't snore, but, for some reason, he became a professional at it last night. His head hung back against his seat on the plane, his mouth hanging wide open. That means I haven't had a wink of sleep in the past twenty-four hours.

If that wasn't enough to make me cranky, Mr. Bigfoot stepped on my toes as we got off the plane without realizing it, so I shoved him off with several curse words falling from my lips and my middle finger raised high to flip him off.

I love my brother. He's my favorite person in the entire world, but when I don't get sleep, no one should be around me. Especially not the person who prevented me from getting my eight hours in. As an aspiring Formula One racer who works out almost every single day, I need rest to let my muscles rejuvenate.

Adrian's been walking behind me for a while now, keeping his distance, asking why the hell I'm limping. I don't dignify his question with an answer, merely continue making my way out of the airport so we can go... *home*.

After a couple more minutes of me silently walking ahead, I take a deep breath and turn around only to realize he's disappeared.

"Adrian!" I hiss, hoping he will hear me. He appears in front of me with a smug smile on his face moments after I first called out his name and probably made a fool of myself spinning in circles to find him.

"You look like a lost child," my brother says, laughing at his joke.

"Where the hell were you?" He cocks an amused brow at me, smiling like he always does before he says something that'll make me want to punch him in the arm.

"I told you I had to pee, but you were too busy pouting to notice. I'm pretty sure the whole airport knew where I was, except for you, Ms. I'm-limping-for-no-apparent-reason." The smirk that follows his words only intensifies my irritation with him.

I need to get some sleep, and *soon*.

"Ten, nine, eight, seven..." I count down, enunciating each number and probably spitting in his face. When I finally reach "one," I take a deep breath. "Taxi?" I ask with the fakest smile and a chipper tone.

Adrian wipes my saliva from his face with an unimpressed look but follows me toward the taxi line outside the airport.

"Grandpa's house isn't too far from here," he informs me for the third time today after telling the driver where to go. I know exactly where the house is, but he's nervous, and when Adrian's nervous, he repeats himself and points out obvious things.

I nod absentmindedly, closing my eyes and only opening them once we're in Monaco, my attention drifting out of the window. The Mediterranean Sea is captivating. The landscape is just as breathtaking as I remember it, sending guilt through me for not coming back sooner. Guilt for being unable to work past my grief enough to come back.

I never thought I would return to Monaco after everything that happened. It was my home for so long, but when I was ripped from it when everyone I ever loved here was ripped from me too, I couldn't imagine living here ever again.

But not even my grief is strong enough to get rid of the homesick feeling that's been camping out in my stomach for the years I lived in L.A. Not even my grief was strong enough to make me stay with my aunt.

My heart is here, in the old yet highly valuable buildings. In the harbor filled with yachts and other boats. In the cafés and restaurants that serve overpriced food because Monaco is one of the most expensive countries in the world. In the people who have always been so kind and adventurous here. I belong here, to the roads I walked with my grandfather when I was a kid. I belong to the streets where he taught me everything I know. I belong to the place where my heart and soul feel at home.

I close my eyes again when tears shoot into them, hoping it'll help keep my emotions at bay. Nostalgia combined with grief makes breathing almost impossible.

When we pull into my grandfather's driveway, I suck in a sharp breath without meaning to. This house represents family. My family. Adrian and I spent most of our childhood here, learning our manners, how to read and write, take care of ourselves, excel at racing, and who we are.

"Valentina."

Adrian's voice brings me back to reality, but his hand waving in front of my face doesn't. I slap it away and glare at him, but he reaches it out again and, suddenly, there's a compassionate look on his face. My brother wipes away my involuntary tears and forces a smile.

"I know. I miss them, too," he admits, leaning toward me and placing a swift kiss against my temple, hugging me to his chest to give me comfort and take some from me, too.

Grandfather's house seems bigger than I remember it. The white columns at the front of it, including the stone facade, are still the same ones my grandparents had used to build the house. What people consider the backyard is actually next to the driveway of the house. The only thing separating them is a carefully crafted barrier of stone that reaches my hips. There's a gate that needs to be opened to drive into the driveway too, ensuring no one can come in without permission.

The veranda leads to a grass area and the pool, and as I study it all, taking in the house that always felt more like a home than my father's place, I feel my heart drop from the overwhelming pain that always comes with my grief.

Grandfather left us his home five years ago when he died of lung cancer. Until now, Adrian and I haven't been able to come back, but six months ago, we decided to renovate it and move in.

The familiar smell of roses and freshly watered plants hits my nose. The sun burns my skin. I take off my flip-flops before I step onto the grass near the veranda and let the feeling of the slightly wet, cold grass envelop my feet. They carry me toward the large front door, which Adrian and the taxi driver patiently wait for me to unlock.

We carry the luggage inside and put it in the foyer, handing the taxi driver the money before he leaves again.

The antique chandelier hanging from the high ceiling catches my attention, reminding me of the day my grandfather explained to me what a "chandelier" is.

"Val, are you okay?" Adrian asks when I don't move or talk. I nod and feel his hand on my shoulder before he squeezes it comfortingly. My eyes move to the glass doors leading to the kitchen, the living room, and the dining room.

"Are *you* okay?" I ask him when he studies our house in the same way I am.

"Yes, I'm just feeling a little nostalgic, I guess," he admits as he runs his hand through his curly, dirty blonde hair with a nervous laugh.

Adrian and I look a lot alike, too much alike for siblings with a four-year age gap. Our hair is the same color; our eyes are the same combination of green, blue, and a little bit of brown. He and I have the same set of straight teeth, round lips, and small ears. However, I'm pretty short and curvy while Adrian is the complete opposite.

Many people think he's too tall to drive in a Formula One car, but he proves them wrong with every race he wins. Adrian is a young championship contender at merely twenty-three years of age, but he's a fantastic racer, just like our father and grandfather were.

When I first asked my grandfather what Formula One was, he said, "It's a fast-paced racing sport with twenty drivers competing in the championship. The cars race around unique tracks at a speed of over three hundred kilometers per hour. A specific number of laps have to be completed within a two-hour window for each track, and whoever crosses the finish line first wins. The race weekends are held from Friday to Sunday, with press events and fan meet and greets on Thursdays. The main event is the race, the Grand Prix, on Sunday. The sport was founded in the UK, and more than half of the races take place in Europe, making it very Eurocentric."

It was so technical, my four-year-old brain only understood a few words, but he kept repeating it, kept saying the same thing over and over until I understood not just the words, but what they meant put together that way.

He helped me study the team names too. There are ten teams in total: Spark Racing, Grenzenlos, Hawke Racing, Aerodinámica, Carousel Racing, Tempête Racing, Zeitgeist Racing, Klein Racing, and Velocità Rossa. I haven't forgotten any names since he told me.

"Want to go out with me tonight? I'm meeting up with some of the other drivers," Adrian offers, and I smile.

As competitive as all of them are, the drivers still make up a tight-knit community.

"Who is coming?" I ask, trying to hide the curiosity I feel spreading across my face.

"James, Leonard, Cameron, and Gabriel."

Gabriel Biancheri...

My heart beats faster against my ribcage, but I hide my excitement. Gabriel Biancheri is the goofiest, most compassionate, and most gorgeous guy I've ever seen. For more than two years, I've had the biggest crush on the Monegasque. He is kind, intelligent, and an incredible racing driver. We've been friends since we met a little over two years ago at a dinner party Adrian invited me to. It was to help me make connections in the Formula One world, to get my name out there.

As soon as I saw Gabriel across the room, I couldn't look away anymore. He was just so... breathtaking. Mesmerizing.

"Okay, what time?" I ask, trying to stop my heart from racing from excitement.

"Seven o'clock," he replies and follows me into the kitchen.

The kitchen has a modern electric stove in the middle connected to an island, which has three brown leather chairs standing against it. There are brown, wooden cabinets all over the walls, and an oven and a microwave on the left. My eyes drift to the clock by the oven to see it's only two in the afternoon.

"What do you think we should do?" he asks, so I look up at my brother.

"It may be better to go grocery shopping since we both haven't eaten much in the past twenty-four hours," I tell Adrian as my stomach growls, and he winks knowingly at me. A grin spreads over his face, so I furrow my brows, unsure what the look is for.

"Excited to see the cars?"

Realization washes over me before I almost jump up and down in excitement. Adrian leads me toward the garage before opening the door and letting me step through it first.

My heart explodes into a million pieces at the sight in front of us. A black 1955 Chevrolet Bel Air stands at the front of the garage, followed by a blue 1973 Ford Mustang. However, Grandfather possessed more than just classic cars. He also bought a white 2014 Audi Q7 and a gray 2014 BMW X6 before he died. I love those cars, both classic and new, although nothing will ever come close to the adrenaline rush I feel when I see an F1 car.

"Which one?" Adrian asks. I point at the Mustang without hesitating.

With a simple smile, he gets the key and throws it to me. Thanks to years of reflex training in preparation for racing in Formula One, I catch them with ease. Without wasting any time, I get into the baby blue car. My fingers run over the black leather steering wheel, and I sigh when my eyes drift to the air refresher hanging from the inside mirror. It was the first one my grandfather had ever gotten. He always kept it there as a good luck charm, even after the scent faded.

My heart is pounding, and my right knee shakes as I turn on the engine of the first car I ever drove.

After our trip to the grocery store, I head upstairs and unpack my things. The walls in my old bedroom are a soothing, light blue color. My curtains are thick and dark, and my golden brown wooden bed stands in the middle of the left wall.

I finish unpacking within an hour, making sure to put all my pictures on my nightstand and sitting down at the foot of my bed to study the art Grandfather chose not too long ago. The painting of the last Formula One car Dad drove, a much smaller version of Adrian's Velocità Rossa this year, stares back at me, and my mind drifts to him.

A memory I have been suppressing since the day he died appears in my head, and I let it consume me.

***

"Daddy, how fast can you go?" I look up at my father, a bright smile appearing on his face. We're walking past tall people who wear all different kinds of colors. I see blue, yellow, and green. My dad says all teams have a different color, but my favorite is the one he is wearing: red.

"Very fast. At our fastest, almost three hundred kilometers per hour," Daddy explains, and I stare at him, completely mesmerized. My daddy stops walking when someone starts talking to him.

I wait impatiently for the woman to leave him alone so I can ask my next question.

"Can I drive one?" He only shakes his head. His blonde hair hides underneath a hat, which has a picture of a black horse on it. Dad calls it the Velocità Rossa symbol, but I call it "Champion," like my daddy.

"It's too dangerous for children. When you're older and become the strong woman I know you will be, you can drive one," he assures me, but I pout anyway. I want to drive one right now.

My dad leads me to the bright red car. He allows me to touch it. My tiny fingers run over the smooth metal, and I jump when I feel how cold it is. I lift my eyes to look at Dad again, but he is talking to a different person. Even though it's really cold, I leave my hand on the car and tilt my head to the side. It's much bigger than the one I sit in when Grandpa takes me karting. It has a long, pointy nose with a mustache at the front, reminding me a bit of my grandpa. It gets bigger where the cockpit is. Adrian calls it the belly, but I like the word "cockpit" better because my daddy and all his friends at work use it. Another word I like is "wing," and it's behind the cockpit. It is the tallest part of the car, a lot taller than me.

I pull on my daddy's arm.

"Not now, Valentina," he scolds, and I frown. He does this to me a lot.

My eyes go back to the car, and I smile. It's very loud here. I barely heard my dad yell at me before. People run from one side to the other, screaming at each other.

Almost everyone has a serious expression on their face. They look like Adrian when he concentrates really hard on coloring inside the lines. I always tell him he can't do it, and I'm always right. I don't think he likes my coloring books very much.

I bring my eyes back to the car. It must be a lot of fun to sit in it, but I'm never allowed. Dad doesn't want me to break anything, which is why I'm only allowed to touch the nose and mustache. I'm not sure what it's actually called. My dad's best friend stands next to me, so I poke his leg to get his attention.

"What is that thing?" I point at the mustache. At first, he seems confused, but then he gives me that same weird smile many adults give me.

"That is called a front wing. It makes sure the airflow is redirected so the car can go faster. With the shape of the car and its light weight, it needs a–" He stops, and I blink cluelessly at him. "Uhm, how can I explain it to you? The air goes... swoosh." I nod, although I still don't get it. My eyes stay on the car.

"I'm going to drive you one day," I whisper right before my dad pulls me away.

Continued in Rush: Part One & Two *also by Bridget L. Rose.*

Acknowledgements

Writing this novella made me realize just how much I love each and every single one of my characters. It made me realize that the found family trope is by far one of my favorite tropes in the world because, no matter what, these characters are always there for each other. So, I want to thank them all. I want to thank them for reminding me why I love writing. Why I started in the first place.

I also want to thank Drew for "bullying" me into writing this novella (Drew's words, not mine). I'm so grateful for your never-ending love and support.

Most importantly, as always, I want to thank my sister. I couldn't have asked for a better business partner. Thank you for spending hours making the interior, fixing the covers, and doing everything I ask you to do. I know I can be annoying with all of my ideas and everything I want us to do, so I'm very grateful you're patient and make those visions come true.

And to all of my bookstagram/booktok friends, thank you for being the most amazing people in the world. I'd be nowhere without you all.

About the Author

Bridget L. Rose is a half-German, half-Italian author, who was born and raised in Germany until the age of thirteen. She fell in love with books from a young age, and soon discovered her passion for writing as well. She likes to spend her free time with her family, reading a book, or writing one herself. She also adores the sport Formula One, which led her to write her Pitstop Series.

Books by Bridget L. Rose

The Pitstop Series

Jump-Start

**The Inside
of a Rainbow**

**Rush:
Part One & Two**

**Chase:
Part One & Two**

Reserved

**The Last
Championship
(Novella)**

From Angels to Devils Series

From Devils to Angels